VENGEANCE RIDER

Sam Wallace had left Grant City because he was tired of always being outshone by his brother Joel, whose election as sheriff had been the last straw as far as Sam was concerned. Two years had passed, during which time Sam had not written a single word to the banker's daughter whom he had loved and left behind. So he could not be too surprised, even though he was downcast, by the news that she was marrying the lawman. Sam came back to attend the wedding and then be on his way again. But the bridegroom was shot dead on the very steps of the church, and Sam decided he'd better stick around awhile to settle matters.

[illegible]

[illegible] was tired of always being [illegible] by his brother [illegible] decided [illegible] had seen [illegible] as [illegible] as [illegible] [illegible] which [illegible] [illegible] the [illegible] daughter [illegible] had loved and [illegible] he could not be [illegible] enough [illegible] [illegible] that [illegible] was [illegible] the [illegible] wedding and the [illegible] [illegible] [illegible] the [illegible] [illegible] [illegible] [illegible]

VENGEANCE RIDER

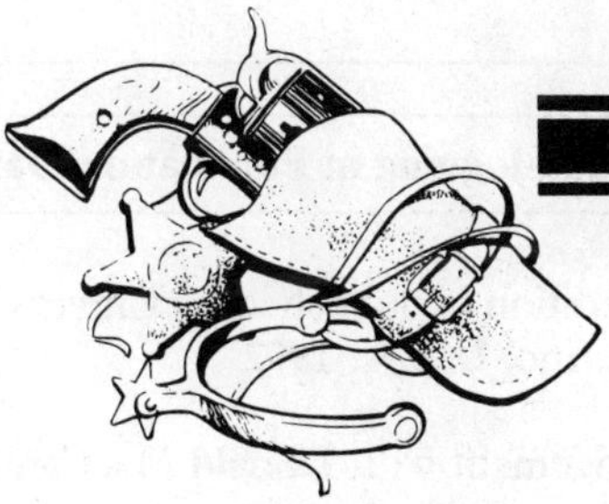

Dan Roberts

Chivers Press, Bath, England.
Curley Publishing, Inc.,
Hampton, N.H., U.S.A.

Library of Congress Cataloging-in-Publication Data

Roberts, Dan, 1912–
Vengeance rider / by Dan Roberts.
p. cm.—(Atlantic large print)
"An Atlantic book."
ISBN 0–7451–8424–3 (lg. print).—ISBN 0–7451–8429–4 (softback : lg. print).—ISBN 0–7927–1342–7 (Curley : softback : lg. print)
1. Large type books. I. Title.
PR9199.3.R5996V39 1992
813′.54—dc20 82–17064
CIP

British Library Cataloguing in Publication Data available

This Large Print edition is published by Chivers Press, England, and Curley Publishing, Inc, U.S.A. 1992

Published by arrangement with Donald MacCampbell, Inc.

U.K. Hardback ISBN 0 7451 8424 3
U.K. Softback ISBN 0 7451 8429 4
U.S.A. Softback ISBN 0 7927 1342 7

Photoset, printed and bound in Great Britain by
REDWOOD PRESS LIMITED, Melksham, Wiltshire

To Anne and Jerry Peer, Frances and Bob Lee,
John and Nancy Ross.

VENGEANCE RIDER

CHAPTER ONE

It was just after nine on a warm June evening when Sam Wallace pushed his way through the swinging doors of the Longhorn Saloon. No one seemed to notice his tall, slim figure as he hesitated for a moment just inside. His thoughtful, tanned face was prematurely lined for a man only in his late twenties, and there was a stern gleam in his narrowed blue eyes. It seemed to him the saloon was as noisy and crowded as ever. Moss Jackson, cigarette dangling from thin lips, still sat on the small stage at the rear, beating out ragtime on an indifferent piano; and Lean Jim Slade, the saloon's proprietor and Grant City's big-time gambler, was conducting a game at a table of six.

A glance in the direction of the bar that ran the length of the long room on the left revealed a few vacant spots near the rear. The young ranch foreman made his way around the crowded tables toward the bar. He was somewhat startled by the number of new faces in the place. If the saloon remained the same, the patrons had not. In the two years of his absence from Grant City, he'd heard a lot of newcomers had settled in the town, and it seemed the rumor was well-founded.

He took his place at the bar, and a rotund

bald bartender moved down the line to serve him. At once the barkeep's fat face took on a smile.

'Good to see you, Sam!' the bartender said. 'Back for the wedding, I reckon?'

Sam offered the beaming man a thin smile in return. 'That's it,' he agreed. 'Whiskey double.'

The bartender nodded. 'The usual,' he said, anxious to let Sam know he remembered.

As the young ranch foreman waited for his drink, he let his eyes lift to the painting of a buxom, dark-haired woman stretched out on a chaise longue that decorated the wall directly above him. A twinkle showed in his sober blue eyes. At least this was one old friend he recognized, one female who had remained faithful and waited for him. It was too bad he couldn't say the same for Virginia Cameron. Virginia was marrying his brother Joel tomorrow. But then he supposed he had no cause to be bitter. He had struck out from Grant City on his own and left his brother Joel an open field with Virginia, so it was no wonder she had transferred her affections to him, especially after Sam had deliberately neglected to write during the time he was away. He'd left Grant City right after Joel had been elected sheriff. Joel, his more successful older brother, somehow always made him feel like a failure. It had been Joel's election as sheriff that had decided him. He wanted to go somewhere where he could make a career on his own and not always be regarded as Joel Wallace's younger brother. He had tried to make a tearful Virginia understand when he'd talked it over with her on the night before he left, but he guessed he hadn't done a very good job.

'Double whiskey, Sam!' the bartender slid the drink in front of him with a flourish.

He nodded. 'Thanks!' And then, like a man who had been on the trail too long and whose throat was parched with heat and dust, he quickly drained the glass. As the burning fluid trickled down his gullet, he could feel some of his tenseness leave him. He pushed the empty glass across to be filled again.

He drank harder these days. Somehow it seemed part of the new life he'd been living since he'd gone south. Back there he had won a place for himself as a first rate ranch foreman, and nobody worried about who his brother was. He liked the cattle country and intended to go back as soon as the wedding was over. It was scheduled for tomorrow morning, and he was to be best man. That was why he had returned to Grant City for this brief period. If all went well, he'd light out for the south tomorrow afternoon. There was nothing for him here but bitter memories.

Just as the bartender refilled his glass and

he was about to lift it to his lips, he felt a newcomer push in beside him and glanced quickly to his right to find himself looking down at a skinny, woebegone little man with the thin purple face and bulbous veined nose of the problem drinker.

'Am I in time for a quick one with you?' the little man asked with the air of one who didn't expect to be refused.

'You bet you are!' Sam said heartily, and signaled the bartender to look after the newcomer. With an expression of distaste, the fat man put down another glass and a bottle of bourbon.

'Thank you, my friend,' the little man said with exaggerated politeness, and proceeded to pour himself a stiff one from the tall bottle. 'It's good to rest a foot on a rail beside you, Sam.'

'Good to see you, Soak,' he told the little man. 'I asked Joel about you first thing.' This was true. Soak Dooley had been one of the few people he'd inquired about since his arrival. He'd always been fond of the little man, whose only fault had been that he drank too much. At one time Soak had been deputy sheriff, but Joel ruefully had told of the many instances when the little man had let him down and of finally having to let him go.

After they had drained their drinks and Soak had poured himself another, Sam asked, 'What are you doing now, Soak?'

The purple face took on an ashamed look under the battered Stetson. 'Joel told you about me,' Soak said.

'He did.'

'I guess I was a sure enough cactus under his saddle,' the little man said, studying his drink mournfully. 'He done right to fire me.' He shrugged. 'I was tired of the law, anyhow. Since then I've been a cowhand at the Circle 3, at least part of the time.'

Sam studied him shrewdly. 'I hear ranching is on the way out in this part of the country.'

Soak showed his disgust. 'You're sure as shootin' right,' he declared. 'The farmers are moving in every day.' He waved a hand to take in the crowded room behind them. 'You must have noticed how many strangers there are here. It's the same everywhere! Soon as they found out Turkey Red wheat could be raised here, they started to settle down.'

'How does Jim Halliday feel about that?' Sam asked, naming the owner of the Circle 3, who had the largest spread in the district.

Soak finished off half his drink and then regarded the glass with a sour expression. 'He's right angered,' he said. 'There's been a lot of hard feelings, and Ben ain't helped things any.' Ben was the son of the owner of the Circle 3, and Sam remembered him as a typical spoiled wealthy young man. He now recalled that Ben had once also shown a lot of interest in brown-haired Virginia Cameron, who would be a bride tomorrow. Virginia had attracted all the eligible young men in Grant City at one time or another.

'Cattle ranching is still strong in the south,' Sam said. 'Which is lucky for me, since I've found myself a good foreman's job.'

'So I heard,' Soak said with a show of genuine pleasure on his thin face with its stubble of gray beard. 'You were wise to get away from here.' The last was said in a low voice, as if the former deputy sheriff had a special reason for making the comment. His remark and manner of saying it made Sam's eyebrows lift.

'Whenever times are bad,' he said, 'there is bound to be unrest.'

'Began with the grasshopper plague in '74,' Soak said. 'And since then it's been either drought or depression or both! And on top of that there's been a rash of cattle rustling that the sheriff don't seem to be able to do anything about.'

This was news to Sam. He stared at the little man. 'It's the first I've heard about it.'

Soak Dooley glanced around cautiously as if to make sure they wouldn't be overheard and then leaned closer to Sam. 'Started soon after you left here,' he said in a low voice. 'The Circle 3 has been hit worst. Jim Halliday is blaming Joel for not stopping the rustling. Seems a lot of cattle have been showing up in

Abilene stockyards with a Cactus 8 brand.' The little man paused significantly. 'Only there don't happen to be any Cactus 8 outfit in this state. The way Jim Halliday figures it, it ain't hard to switch a C3 brand to a C8. And that's the way it stands.'

Sam was puzzled. 'Doesn't Joel have any idea who might be to blame?' he asked.

The little man shrugged. 'He's got some suspicions. Remember Bull Bender?'

Sam recalled the big hulking man with the livid scar of some ancient gun battle running directly across the middle of his forehead; a town bully who had spent his share of time in the city jail. Bull Bender had never pretended to have any regular job, and everyone in the area thought him an outlaw.

Sam said, 'Bender sounds like a good candidate. But would he have the brains to operate a rustling set-up?'

'Joel is plumb puzzled about that,' Soak said. 'He thinks there is somebody back of him. But he figures Bull is the head of the gang that does the actual rustling.'

'Looks as if there is more excitement in Grant City than I thought,' Sam said with a thin smile, and nodded to the bartender to set up drinks for them again. 'What ever happened to Barney Wales?'

'He went off to try his hand at mining,' Soak said with disgust. 'Crazy idea, I call it! And he's gotten real queer for a young fella!

Comes into town now and then for provisions, but never stays long. And I guess he don't bother to stop to talk to Joel any more, though they were the best of friends.'

'I remember,' Sam replied. He recalled Barney Wales as a handsome, thick-set young man with a lot of blond hair. He couldn't picture the good-natured youth as a recluse miner, working in the hills and avoiding the town and his former friends.

He was about to question Soak about some other people when he felt a hand on his shoulder. Instinctively his own hand reached down for the Colt in his holster. Then he wheeled around quickly to find himself face to face with a broad-shouldered, well-dressed young man with a square, florid face. It was a sneering Ben Halliday who had come up behind him.

'Back for the wedding?' was his mocking question.

'That's right,' Sam said evenly. He had never been an admirer of the spoiled youth. 'You sound as if you might have some objections.'

Ben Halliday laughed nastily. 'Not about you,' he said. 'But I happen to believe the wedding is a mistake. Virginia must be a fool to throw herself away on a sheriff who isn't even able to do his job right!'

Sam's thin face was expressionless. 'Have you told Joel that?' he asked.

Ben Halliday looked a little less sure of himself. 'I will when I see him,' he said.

'I'd do that,' Sam told him in a cutting tone. 'It might be you'd get some very interesting results.' He saw the thin, dark-clothed figure of gambler Lean Jim Slade coming quickly toward them.

The saloon owner's high-cheek-boned face wore a grim expression. His cold eyes fixed on Sam. 'It doesn't take long to find out you're back,' he said. 'If you're looking for trouble, I'd appreciate you going somewhere else.'

Sam nodded toward Ben Halliday. 'Better save that advice for your card-playing friend here,' he said. Lean Jim Slade flushed angrily, for it was well known that Ben lost plenty at the Longhorn's gambling table.

Ben made a fast move toward his gun belt, but Lean Jim Slade was even quicker as he reached to intercept his angry reaction. The gambler spoke urgently. 'This is no time to settle differences, Ben!'

The lumbering youth hesitated, his face a mottled red. 'Okay, Jim,' he said. And then to Sam he added, 'Don't think I won't be on the lookout for you!'

'I'll be around for at least another twenty-four hours,' Sam said, his blue eyes leveling on him.

'That will be long enough,' Ben warned him. Then the gambler took him by the arm and led him back in the direction of the big table.

'Well, that's over with!' Soak Dooley said, giving a sigh of relief that was clearly audible. 'Looked to me as if you might celebrate your homecoming with a gunfight.'

'I don't want any kind of celebration,' Sam said; 'certainly not a gun battle on the night before the wedding.' He was acutely conscious of the many curious eyes still on him. 'Let's get out of here,' he told the little man, and at the same time reached in his pocket for the money for the drinks and threw it on the counter.

It was a pleasant change to leave the hot, smoke-filled air of the saloon for the pleasant coolness of the June night. The hitching rail in front of the Longhorn was crowded with the horses of celebrants inside. The wooden sidewalks of the small city's main street were busy, and every few minutes a wagon or a rider passed on the way in or out of town. From across the street and a little farther down, there came a roar of hilarity as a gang of noisy cowpokes emerged from the cattle town's other main saloon, the Grant City.

Soak Dooley grinned up at Sam as they stood there and said, 'Surely you won't miss stopping by and saying hello to Laura?'

Sam hesitated before replying.

The friendship between Laura Thorpe and himself dated back to the period when they were teen-agers in Grant City. Laura had always been a high-spirited, strong-willed girl with a startling beauty to match a lovely creamy complexion and flaming red hair. Sam smiled to himself as he thought of how quickly Laura had grown up. It seemed she had always been falling in and out of love with someone. For a while he had been her choice, and then it was his brother Joel who seemed to have captured her heart.

Yet in the end she had surprised them all by marrying Bruce Thorpe, the elderly, wealthy proprietor of the Grant City Saloon. Thorpe had lived only a year after the marriage. Laura nursed him through a stroke and was a faithful wife to him until he died. After that she had left Grant City for a spell. It was said she'd decided to sell the saloon and remain in the East. Instead she had showed up again shortly, decked out in smart city clothes and looking more beautiful than ever. The young widow had settled down to running the saloon and, though many of the town's Romeos made a play for her hand, she no longer seemed interested in romance or marriage.

'I suppose I should stop and see her a minute,' Sam mused.

'Surest thing you know!' Soak Dooley chuckled. 'And I could sure do with another bourbon.'

So it was that a few minutes later they were

installed at the bar of the Grant City Saloon. It was not as crowded as the Longhorn, but there were enough at the bar and around the scattered tables to give the house a good profit. It wasn't until after they'd ordered drinks that Laura Thorpe came out of her office in the rear of the big room and spied Sam standing at the bar.

With a loud whoop of joy, she ran down the length of the room and threw herself in Sam's arms.

'You big galoot!' she exclaimed. 'I've missed you!'

Sam laughed. 'I can see that! The place is so quiet!'

'All this is business,' she said with a wistful expression on her pretty face. 'I'm really a lonely widow!'

'You'll have a hard time convincing me of that,' Sam said. He was impressed by her expensive low-cut green dress, the string of pearls at her throat and the tall colorful plume fastened in her flaming hair to give her a striking, regal quality.

'Come on back to the office for a while so we can talk,' Laura begged.

Sam glanced uncomfortably at Soak Dooley and said, 'I mean to get back to the house early. Joel may be wanting me for something. And I have Soak here as my guest.' The little man smiled at Laura over his bourbon.

'He'll be my guest while we gossip,' Laura

insisted. And with a nod to the bartender, 'Give Soak as much as he can hold!'

'You're sure lettin' yourself in for a loss, ma'am,' Soak warned her with a delighted chuckle.

Laura waved his remark aside and, taking Sam's arm, led him toward the door marked, 'Manager, Private.' He noted the knowing glances of the cowpokes at the tables as they passed and figured he would be marked as a long-lost beau of the attractive saloon owner.

In the office, Laura waved him to a chair. 'Sit down,' she ordered, 'while I pour you a drink.'

She sat opposite him, her big green eyes shining with excitement. 'It is good to see you in town again. Plan to stay long?'

'Only for the wedding,' he said. 'I aim to hit the road late tomorrow afternoon.'

Her face was somber. 'You don't care much for this town or your friends here.'

'There's nothing here for me now,' he said, before he realized that he had been too brutally frank. With an apologetic smile, he added, 'I'm not referring to grand ladies way beyond my reach.'

It was her turn to smile faintly. 'What makes you think any one of them wouldn't be happy to have you as her man?'

He gulped down half his drink. Then he said, 'Because I've always been able to judge myself with a clear eye. It isn't always pleasant, but it keeps me from getting any crazy ideas.'

'Love is always a crazy idea,' she reminded him. 'And that's what I think about this wedding tomorrow. I can't figure a man like Joel tying himself up to a meek-mouthed little creature like Virginia Cameron. Forgetting she's the banker's daughter, what can he see in her?'

Sam was surprised at the vehemence of Laura's tone. He said, 'Virginia's a fine girl! If you knew her better, you would understand why Joel is lucky to get her as a wife.'

'She's not the sort of person I want to know,' Laura said with a touch of bitterness. 'Of course her dear father wouldn't allow her to set foot in a place like this, though I was sent an invitation to the wedding. I suppose that was Joel's doing.'

Sam knew this was likely, but he said, 'I am sure they both want you to be there.'

'I'll be there all right,' Laura said with a strange veiled expression. 'I wouldn't dream of missing it. I guess everyone will expect my heart to be broken.' She sighed. 'I've carried the torch for that handsome brother of yours far too long.'

Sam said, 'You've had a happy marriage of your own. Why should anyone think that?'

Laura's lip curled as she gave him a bitter smile. 'Marrying Bruce Thorpe wasn't exactly an act of love. I knew he had plenty of cash, an eye for young girls, and not too good health.'

The frank cynicism on the lovely young woman's part shocked Sam. He said quietly, 'You made him a good enough wife.'

'Sure I did,' Laura agreed. 'I'm the kind that always keeps a bargain. And so is Joel. That's why he'll stick with that little Cameron girl even when he finds out the marriage is a mistake.'

'What makes you so sure it will be?'

Her keen eyes met his. 'Just take my word for it,' she said. 'A lot of things have been happening here since you left. There has been a heap of trouble, and Joel has been in the middle of it. You've heard about the rustling of the Circle 3 stock?'

He nodded. 'Yes. Not much, but enough to know what you're talking about.'

'Joel may not be sheriff much longer,' Laura warned. 'The Hallidays are after him. They're working on the mayor to bring in outside law. And I hear Ben Halliday was mooning after Virginia Cameron before Joel cut him out, so that's a Halliday with a double grudge against him.'

'Joel is a born lawman,' Sam said carefully. 'I'd be willing to bet he'll clear up this rustling before long. Like as not he's already got a good idea who is to blame.'

Laura gave him a knowing glance. 'I'm

willing to agree with you, because I think Joel is among the best. But I doubt if you'd find many others in Grant City who share your views.'

Sam stood up. 'I'll see you at the wedding, then.'

'Sure,' she said, rising to see him out. 'I suppose you're to be the best man?'

He smiled. 'That's the reason I came all the way up from the south.'

Laura Thorpe opened the door to the saloon. 'Too bad it couldn't have been for a better cause,' she said with a sigh.

Soak Dooley had been taking full advantage of Laura's generous offer and was pretty far gone by the time Sam joined him. The little man swayed slightly as he removed his battered Stetson and bowed low to Laura before they left. Sam took him by the arm and led him firmly to the exit.

Outside, the cool air seemed to revive the little man. 'I better ride to the house with you, Sam,' he said. 'After that run-in with Halliday, you don't know who might be waitin' for you around a dark corner.'

'Don't worry about me,' Sam told him. 'You're the one I'm concerned about. Can you make it to your place?'

The little man drew himself up with pathetic dignity. 'I may be drunk, but my horse is stone sober,' he said. 'She may be a ornery old nag, but she always restores me to the bosom of my family.'

Sam was forced to laugh. He saw the little man safely on the sway-backed chestnut mare, and after they were on their way he swung into the saddle of his own roan and headed for the white frame house with its surrounding picket fence on the street that ran parallel with the main street. It was where he and Joel had grown up, with only a widowed mother to take care of them. When their mother had died, an aunt had come to take over as housekeeper, and the spinster sister of their father's had remained there ever since. Tomorrow would be a big day for her. Sam was certain she had spent long hours cleaning the house and cooking special delicacies for the occasion.

As he neared the house, he saw the lights were on in the living room and did not find this strange, even though the hour was now late. He'd had an idea Joel might wait up to see him. No doubt his brother wanted to go over the last minute details.

Sam took the horse around back and settled it down for the night. By the time he'd removed its saddle and seen it had a drink, quite a few minutes had passed. As he strode quickly toward the front door of the white frame house in the darkness, he noticed the gray horse tethered by the fence. Evidently Joel had a caller.

As he came up to the door, he was startled

to hear loud, angry voices coming from inside. One of them belonged to Joel, and the other he recognized as that of Virginia's father, Charles Cameron, the Grant City banker.

Charles Cameron sounded enraged as he declared, 'In view of this note, I am not sure that I should allow you to marry my daughter at all.'

CHAPTER TWO

Sam stood in the darkness for a moment with his hand on the doorknob. He hesitated to intrude on the unhappy scene between the two men. Yet he knew they must have heard him ride up a few minutes before and would be expecting him to appear. So he opened the door and stepped inside. Joel and the banker were in the living room, facing one another with scowling faces.

As soon as Joel saw him, his expression became less angry and he came out to the hall to meet him. 'I'm glad you're here, Sam,' he said in a quiet voice. 'I've run into some trouble.'

Pretending he hadn't heard anything, Sam said, 'Oh?'

Now banker Charles Cameron came out to the living room doorway. He was a dumpy man with a bald head over which a few black hairs had been carefully brushed. He had a puffy jowled face, with deep-set eyes that looked like cold black currants now.

He raised a pudgy hand in protest. 'I don't think we need wash our dirty linen before your brother,' he said.

Joel Wallace gave him a reproving glance. He was a handsome young man, as tall as Sam but more filled out. His hair was also a shade more sandy, and he had an air of aggressiveness lacking in Sam.

He said, 'If we do as you say, the whole town will know we're having trouble. I think we should take Sam into our confidence now.'

The banker glowered unhappily. 'Well, if you must!'

Joel turned to Sam again. 'Mr. Cameron received a note tonight that upset him,' he said. 'In fact, he came here to suggest that we postpone the wedding. I think the whole thing is crazy. The note is from some crackpot who hasn't signed it and blames me for the rustling that is going on.'

'He doesn't blame you,' the banker corrected him. 'He says you are a part of it.'

'The same thing,' Joel said with a shrug.

'I disagree,' Charles Cameron said testily. 'The note suggests that you are closing your eyes to the rustling. And as you well know, a lot of other people in town have been hinting the same thing. Jim Halliday of the Circle 3 has even told the mayor he thinks you're in on the deal.'

'Do you expect Jim Halliday to be fair about this?' Joel asked.

'The rustling has cost him a heap of cash,' the banker said.

Sam was shocked by the banker's bitterness toward Joel. 'Isn't it usually the sheriffs who take the blame when things like this go on a long while?' he asked. 'And don't crackpots of one sort or another generally send in wild letters to the lawmen?'

'This letter was sent to me,' Charles Cameron said stiffly.

'It's no letter,' Joel said. 'It's nothing more than a scrawled note on a dirty sheet of paper, sent in by some trouble-maker. I'll deal with it after the wedding.'

'If there is a wedding,' the banker reminded him.

'As long as Virginia and I haven't changed our minds, I don't think there is much you can do about that, sir,' Joel said.

Sam was glad to see the way his brother handled the situation. And he was quick to add, 'I agree with Joel. You shouldn't think of postponing the wedding.'

The banker hesitated unhappily. 'Virginia is my only daughter. I don't want to risk her future in any way. If you can assure me that you have this rustling business in hand and will clear it up within a short time after the wedding, I'll not refuse my permission.'

'If that is all that's troubling you,' Joel said quietly, 'you have my word. I have been gradually coming closer to the rustling ring. In a fortnight at the most, I hope to be able to make my first arrests.'

Charles Cameron studied him doubtfully; then, with a heavy sigh, he said, 'I hope it will work out that well and that you're not deliberately lying to me.'

And it was on that note that the banker left. Joel waited until he rode off into the night, then closed the door and turned to Sam again. Sam was struck by the sudden weariness in his older brother's face. He was at once aware that the months of tension brought about by the rustling had cost his lawman brother a high price in health.

Joel said, 'Nice situation to break the night before the wedding.'

Sam followed his brother into the living room. 'Cameron has always had a quick, nasty temper,' he reminded Joel. 'How he comes to have a daughter as nice as Virginia I'll never guess.'

Joel slumped into a wing-back chair. 'They say her mother was a wonderful woman. But I suppose you can't really blame Cameron in this case. There have been a lot of dirty rumors, and that note sort of capped them all.'

Sam stared down at his brother's weary,

sprawled-out figure. 'Were you telling him the truth when you said you planned to make some arrests soon?'

'Partly,' Joel said. 'Afraid I was being optimistic.' He paused and looked up at Sam. 'Anyway, I guess the wedding will go on. I can thank you for that. You came at a good time to break up the argument.'

'I think Cameron had begun to realize he was making too much of it.'

Joel frowned. 'You remember Barney Wales?'

'Yes. I was with Soak Dooley tonight, and he said Barney had gone prospecting on his own. Rarely came into town and had gotten kind of odd.'

'Gone clean crazy,' Joel growled. 'That could be closer to the truth. He's working a mine up in the hills that almost certainly will never pay off, and he's a mental case if I ever talked to one. He came into my office for the first time in months about a week ago. He was full of this rustling business and practically told me he knew who was to blame. I aim to ride up and question him some more after the wedding.'

'He's your lead,' Sam said, slightly worried. 'Do you consider him reliable?'

His brother spread his hands in a gesture of despair. 'I have to follow it up. Every other trail has led to a dead end. Barney Wales is my best hope now. He talked in a mixed-up way, but there was something behind his madness. I think he knows enough to help. They may be keeping the stolen cattle near the mine until they move them on to Abilene.'

'I understand there's some fancy brand changing involved,' Sam said.

'That, too,' his brother admitted in a tired voice. And then, forcing a smile, he rose from the chair. 'If I'm going to make any sort of bridegroom, I'd better get some sleep right now.'

By the time Sam came downstairs the next morning, Joel had left for the jail. Aunt Maggie had an old-fashioned breakfast of bacon, eggs and waffles ready for him, and as soon as he'd finished the old woman rushed him out of the house while she and several women friends who had arrived set about getting ready for the reception to be held there later.

Sam was out in the barn when the rider came up with the message from Virginia. It was brief and merely asked him to come to her place at once. She wanted to see him before the wedding. He lost no time saddling the roan and then took the back road to the Cameron homestead, which was on a hill overlooking the town. It was a big house, with white pillars at the entrance. A woman servant answered the door, and when Sam informed her who he was led him to a sitting room to wait for Virginia. The banker's daughter did not take long to join him. And he saw at once that she was upset.

'Sam!' she exclaimed. 'It's so good to have you here now!' And she came close to him.

Sam smiled at her and thought she had never looked more lovely and appealing than she did at that instant in her white dressing gown with her wavy brown hair curling about her shoulders. Again he experienced a moment of pain at the thought that within a few hours she would be lost to him forever. He took her lightly by the arms and drew her to him as he touched his lips gently to her cheek.

'I came as soon as I heard from you,' he said. 'What is wrong?'

Her soft brown eyes searched his face. 'Sam, what is this trouble that has suddenly come up between Joel and my father?'

'Nothing important,' he assured her. 'A misunderstanding. It's settled now.'

'I hope so,' she worried. 'Father was in a rage last night and went out to see Joel about something. This morning he rode over to the Circle 3 Ranch to talk to Jim Halliday, and he should be here getting ready for the wedding.'

'I was at the house when he was there last night,' Sam told her. 'And I know you have nothing to worry about.'

Virginia gave him a rueful smile. 'Why

didn't you ever write me, Sam? I wanted so much to hear from you.'

He raised his eyebrows. 'At first I was waiting to have something to tell you. I wanted to be able to give you the news that I'd built myself a new life. By the time it happened it seemed too late to bother you. I figured you'd probably found somebody else. And you had.'

'It might have been so different if only I'd heard from you,' she said in a tone so soft it was almost a whisper.

Sam was startled by her words. Swallowing hard, he said, 'If there's nothing else, I'd better be getting back to the house. There isn't much time before the wedding.'

'I know,' she agreed.

Arriving at the house, Sam went directly upstairs to his old room. The wedding was only an hour off now, so he began to change into his dark suit and white shirt at once. He had trouble with the black tie, as he'd not had to cope with one for an age. When at last he had it suitably tied, he surveyed himself in the mirror and was satisfied with the results. Glancing at the dresser, he frowned. He had not put on his gun belt but decided it might be a wise precaution. He picked it up and began to buckle it on.

At that moment the door from the hallway opened and Joel, already in his black suit, came into the room. The moment he noticed that Sam was putting on his gun belt, he came toward him.

'No,' he said. 'We're not going to walk up the aisle wearing shooting irons!'

Sam gave him a serious look. 'It seemed it might be a good idea,' he said.

Joel shook his head. 'I'm against it,' he insisted, his hand on the gun belt. 'This is one day I'd like to forget I'm sheriff or there is such a thing as the wrong side of the law.'

'Maybe somebody looking for trouble will turn up at the wedding.'

'Things are bad,' Joel admitted, 'but not that bad. Don't wear your guns, Sam, and I'm not going to be wearing mine.'

Sam sighed and tossed the gun belt back on the dresser. 'It's your wedding day,' he said with a crooked smile.

The Grant City church was a plain gray building without any steeple but boasting a small belfry. As Sam and his brother rode out to the west end of the town where the weathered building stood alone, the bell was already being rung to announce the wedding service. And as they drew near the building, it was plain a good crowd had gathered to see Joel and Virginia married. There were a lot of wagons and carriages in the big yard to the right of the church building and a good many horses tied to the hitching post in the same area.

The sight of a large group of people

clustered around the main entrance to the church and a number of couples already mounting the steps to go in filled Sam with uneasiness. In a crowd like this, anything could happen. Still, it seemed a very orderly gathering, and he could see them through the wedding safely.

In no time he was standing with Joel and Virginia before the venerable minister as he pronounced them man and wife. Sam thought the brown-haired girl looked as beautiful as he'd ever seen her in a flowing white wedding gown and fancy lace veil. There was an appreciative murmur from the crowded benches as the bride and groom kissed. Then Sam was following the two happy newlyweds down the aisle to the door of the church.

Sam stood a foot or so away from the newlyweds, feeling desperately out of place and anxious for the festivities to be over so he could be on his way. Suddenly his attention was attracted to several riders coming down the road from the direction of town at a fast pace. There were three of them, and the pounding hooves of their horses raised a cloud of dust in their wake.

The three riders drew close and Sam's smile vanished as he saw they all were wearing kerchiefs to mask their faces, and each of them carried a drawn gun. By this time everyone on the church steps had noticed the riders, and there were cries of alarm as they scurried for safety. At the same instant the mounted men let loose a barrage of fire that cut Joel down in front of his bride. Sam lunged toward his brother as Joel crumpled swiftly on the steps, a broad splash of red staining the front of his white shirt. By this time the three masked riders had vanished along the road leading out of Grant City, leaving only the unsettled dust rising fitfully in the bright morning sunshine as a reminder of their passage.

Sam was bent over his brother, ignoring the feminine screams and expressions of shock and horror. It took him only a moment to decide Joel was done for, if he was actually still breathing.

'Joel!' he cried, holding the limp body cradled in his arms. 'Joel, can you hear me?'

His brother's answer was to glance up at him feebly with fast glaring eyes. Then, with a great effort, Joel's lips formed the whispered words, 'Barney Wales warned—' But whatever his message was, he never finished it. A slight shiver ran through his body, and his head lolled back. Realizing it was all over, Sam gently lowered the limp figure to the steps and stood up.

Virginia stood facing him, her exquisite white wedding gown a thing of horror now, with its pattern of bloodstains from her husband's wounds. With an ashen face, she gazed at him in terror.

He looked at her forlornly. 'He's gone, Virginia,' he said.

The words had no sooner been uttered than she collapsed. He'd expected this, and so reached out and caught her in his arms.

Then her father came pushing through the horrified onlookers. With an angry glance at Sam, he said, 'I'll take her!' It was more a command than a request, and with a sober look at the older man, Sam transferred Virginia's limp form into his arms. Charles Cameron stalked off in the direction of the wagons, carrying his daughter.

'Them outlaws have gotten a mighty good start on us!' It was Soak Dooley who spoke at Sam's elbow and brought him out of the daze that had followed his brother's murder.

Sam ran the back of his hand across his forehead and realized perspiration was streaming down his face. 'Is the deputy sheriff here?' he asked dully.

Soak shook his head. 'Nope. He didn't come to the wedding.' The little man glared around at the still horrified wedding guests and said scornfully, 'Not a single man of them has tried to follow that gang! Hadn't we ought to do something?'

'I have no gun,' Sam said. 'Joel wanted me to leave it behind for the wedding.' Again he glanced down at his brother's inert form.

'I can rustle you up one in a minute,' Soak assured him. 'I'll go and get the horses.'

The little man ran off, leaving Sam still standing on the steps by Joel's body. A tall, gray-haired man with a pleasant face came up to him. He recognized him as Steve Randall, Grant City's mayor.

The mayor shook his head. 'This is one of the worst things that has ever happened in the town.'

Sam nodded. 'Did anybody recognize who they were?'

'They were masked,' the mayor said. 'I doubt if anyone had time to take much stock of them.' He paused as he stared down at Joel. 'Whoever it was must have hated your brother real bad!'

'A sheriff always makes enemies,' Sam said.

'Not the kind to do a thing like this,' Mayor Steve Randall said heavily. 'To kill a man in cold blood in front of his bride!'

'You better get the deputy on this,' Sam said. 'I'm going to follow their trail.'

The mayor gave him a troubled glance. 'Better not mix into this, Sam. Let the law take care of it. You don't know what you might be letting yourself in for.'

Sam's thin face wore a tight, cold look. 'I haven't got time to wait for the law right now,' he said. 'You look after Joel's body for me.' And with that he went down the steps to join Soak Dooley, who had come up on his own sorry nag, leading Sam's roan. As Sam was about to swing into the saddle, Laura Thorpe came over to intercept him.

'Don't be a fool, Sam,' she told him earnestly. 'You'll never catch up with those three now.'

'I aim to try,' he said, his hand on the bridle knob.

Laura clung to him. 'There's been one killing this morning. Isn't that enough?' she asked. 'Let the law go after them. It's none of your business.'

'What happened to Joel was always my business,' he said grim-faced. 'Sorry, Laura; I don't have any choice about this.' And he pulled free of her and swung lightly into the saddle.

Soak leaned across to deliver a .45 to him. 'The best I could manage,' the little man said.

Sam weighted the weapon. 'It will do,' he said, and nudged the roan into action.

The trail was cold, and all traces of the dust left behind by the hooves of the outlaws' horses had settled, but Sam rode on grimly, following what he believed to be the route they had taken. Somehow Soak Dooley spurred his own broken-down mount and followed only a short distance to the rear of him. It was a grinding pace Sam set in the noonday heat, as the sun burned down mercilessly on them.

He was eventually aware the roan was slowing; he was no longer breathing regularly, but gasping the warm air. A glance behind him told him that Soak had fallen back so that he was barely in sight. It wasn't easy following the wagon road across the rolling plains. At last he came to the crest of a knoll and reined the roan to a halt. He could see for a distance ahead, and there was no sign of the three outlaws he was hunting.

Leaning forward in the saddle in the sweltering heat, he knew that he was defeated. His thin face wore a look of frustration and rage. The realization that he had spurred the roan across the rugged terrain for miles and also tormented his own body to no purpose left him empty and trembling. He was still grimly surveying the horizon when Soak rode up.

The little man brought his mount to a halt. He lifted the battered Stetson to mop his brow. 'Looks like it's no dice, Sam,' he said.

Sam nodded. 'I don't even think they came this way.'

'That's been worrying me for a spell,' Soak agreed. 'I been wanting to ask you. Do you suppose they might have headed for the hill country, up in the direction of Barney Wales' mine?'

Sam gave the little man a sharp glance. 'Could be,' he said. He recalled that Joel's last whispered words had concerned Barney Wales and some warning that had come from the miner.

'Mebbe we should head back to Grant City and find out what is goin' on there,' was Soak's suggestion. 'Could be the deputy has some line of action planned by now.'

'I'd like to think that,' Sam said, 'but I doubt it.' He paused. 'Still, we could question some of the people who were standing in front of the church. Surely somebody got a good enough look at those three to guess who they were.'

'I was standin' real close when they rode up,' Soak said. 'The way they had their faces covered and their hats slouched down, you couldn't see what they looked like. But I'd be willing to bet the big one who rode ahead and acted as leader was Bull Bender.'

Sam frowned at the mention of the outlaw's name. 'You reasonably sure of that?'

'I'd stake a month's liquor on it,' the little man said with a sigh. 'And you know that's a heavy bet for me.'

CHAPTER THREE

The Grant City's sheriff's office was located in the jail house at the opposite end of the town from the church. The one-story building had a verandah across the front and a section of jail cells that jutted out back in a long extension. As they rode up, Sam noted there was a smart carriage hitched out front. He and Soak dismounted, tied their horses to the post and went up the three wooden steps to the verandah and inside.

An elderly, mournful-looking man was seated in a swivel chair in one corner of the sheriff's office. A huge ham-like hand rested on the open surface of a roll-top desk beside him as he stared up at Mayor Steve Randall, who was standing in the center of the big room. Both men gave their attention to Sam and Soak Dooley as they entered.

The mayor spoke first, addressing himself to Sam. 'Any luck?' he asked.

Sam shook his head. 'Reckon we never did follow the right trail.'

'Isn't that what I told you?' the old man in the swivel chair said plaintively. He had a big gray walrus mustache that drooped at the ends and added to the mournful expression of the heavy, lined faced. 'Looking for them is like hunting a needle in a haystack.'

'At least we tried to do something,' Sam said with meaning in his tone. He eyed the man in the chair coldly. 'What has this office done to find the murderers?'

The man with the gray mustache scowled. 'Nothin' yet.'

'That's why I am here,' the mayor said, turning to Sam again. 'This is Deputy Wade Smith. Joel appointed him to office after Soak was let go.'

'Isn't it about time you organized a posse?' Sam asked Deputy Wade Smith. 'Or maybe you want to encourage sheriff killing in the town?'

The old man lifted himself out of the swivel chair and stood glaring at Sam, his fists clenched. 'I don't take that kind of talk from anyone,' he declared.

The mayor waved a placating hand. 'You've got to make some allowance for Sam's feelings right now,' he pointed out. 'It's only a couple of hours since his brother was killed.'

Deputy Wade Smith continued to frown. 'Joel Wallace meant as much to me as he did to any man,' he said. 'And I aim to settle accounts for him in my own way!'

'I'll be interested in seeing how you make out,' Sam said, making it clear he wasn't impressed by the old man's bluster.

Soak Dooley spoke up, asking the mayor, 'What are you going to do about filling the sheriff's job?'

Steve Randall shrugged. 'The job is open. So far I haven't had any one asking for it. The way things are right now, I'd expect it to stay open.'

Sam had been thinking quickly. On an impulse he said, 'If you're on the level about wanting a sheriff, I'll take the job.'

The mayor looked startled. 'You will?'

Sam nodded. 'For a little while, anyhow. I

want to settle things for Joel, and this could be my best way of doing it.'

Deputy Wade Smith gave the mayor an irritable glance. 'Putting him in office is bound to cause more trouble. The same gang that was after his brother would be sure to come gunning for him!'

Sam's cold blue eyes met the deputy's. 'You sound mighty sure of that. Do you know something you're holding back?'

The old man looked startled. 'I don't know anything more than the rest of you, but I can figure out how them outlaws' minds work as well as the next one. Put another Wallace in the sheriff's office, and they'll keep up the feud.'

Mayor Steve Randall's pleasant face showed concern. He glanced from the deputy to Sam. 'You know there could be a lot of truth in what Wade is saying,' he pointed out.

'I'm willing to take any risks that go with the office,' Sam said.

'And I'm ready to offer my services free of charge to the town as a temporary deputy,' Soak Dooley put in, surprising them all.

The mayor's eyebrows rose. 'That's a pretty generous offer from a man in your circumstances, Soak. You sure you wouldn't accept a small drinking allowance, at least?'

'No, sireee!' the little man said defiantly, smacking a fist in his left hand. 'The last thing I need on the job is booze. And if I should get a mite thirsty, I could always call on Sam here to set me up one now and then.'

'Sounds like a satisfactory arrangement,' the mayor said with a gleam of amusement in his normally serious eyes. He glanced at Sam. 'The way I see it, I can get the town the services of an experienced sheriff and deputy without any trouble or delay. It's too good an offer to turn down, Wallace. If you want your brother's star, it's yours!'

'Where do I fit into this?' Deputy Wade Smith asked indignantly.

'I guess you'd stay on as regular deputy and jailer, same as now,' the mayor said. 'Seems like a good arrangement to me.'

'I still say it's askin' for more trouble,' the old deputy grumbled. 'But you're the mayor. I'll go along with whatever you say.'

'Then it's settled,' Mayor Steve Randall said briskly. 'I've got to get back to the bank. I'm mighty sorry about what happened to Joel, and I'll leave you to get things organized here so his killers will be brought to justice!'

'I aim to start working on that right away,' Sam said quietly.

The mayor extended his hand. 'That takes a pile of worry off my mind,' he said. 'Good luck, Sheriff!' And they shook hands.

The mayor left right after that, and Sam sat down with Deputy Wade Smith and began questioning him about what Joel had found out concerning the rustling.

The old man tugged at his gray mustache and seemed to agonize over his answers. The trouble was that none of them added up to anything definite. Soak Dooley sat on a sofa at the other side of the office, his purple face registering disgust.

Deputy Wade Smith smacked a big hand down on his desk despairingly. 'I don't know much about the rustling. Joel was taking care of that on his own. He could keep his mouth shut plenty tight when he liked.'

Sam studied the old man intently, wondering if he might be lying, covering up for someone, or if he was actually as stupid and ill-informed as he pretended. He said, 'Barney Wales came in here to talk to Joel, didn't he? I understand he had some news about the rustling.'

'That one!' Deputy Smith's weathered old face showed disdain. 'He came by a couple of times in the last few months. Crazier than a hoptoad! Just raved on about a lot of stuff that didn't make sense! Joel didn't pay no attention to him.'

'Even if Wales is a little loco, he might have seen something and brought the information to my brother,' Sam said.

'I tell you he's wild-eyed and rambling,' Deputy Smith said. 'Joel didn't get anything from him. Last time, he talked so crazy I just got up and left the office. That Wales is real sick in the head!'

'How far is his mine from here?' Sam wanted to know.

The old deputy glanced across to where Soak Dooley was seated on the sofa. 'You know more about that than me,' he said.

'Mebbe two hours' steady ride,' Soak said. 'It's a rough trail most of the way, and the last stretch is all uphill.'

Sam sat back in his chair. 'If we started out now, we'd have plenty of time to get up there before dark.'

'No trouble on that score,' Soak agreed. Then a canny expression came over his gaunt face. 'But I think you'd do better if you stayed in town now until after the funeral at least.'

Sam frowned. 'But meanwhile those outlaws may be holed up with Barney Wales at the mine.'

'I doubt that,' the little man said. 'Leastways, I doubt if we'd find them if we went up there. The way I see it, you should circulate in town for twenty-four hours or so and let folks see you've taken over Joel's job as sheriff. Once that news gets out, it might just bring Bull Bender and his boys back looking for trouble, like the deputy says.'

Deputy Wade Smith nodded his approval of Soak's comments. 'That's wise advice he's offering you, Sheriff,' the old man said.

Sam got up and, with head bent, began to pace restlessly up and down the office. He said, 'You're asking me just to wait around and see if the killers will come to me. That's not the sort of action I was planning on.'

'This is mighty big country,' Soak reminded him. 'You could waste a heap of time running off in every direction like we did today and getting nothing done beyond tiring ourselves out.'

Sam halted his pacing to give his attention to Deputy Wade Smith. 'Do you remember my brother and Bull Bender having trouble lately?'

'Bull hasn't been in jail for months,' the old deputy said. 'And that's enough to make you think he's up to something big! Your brother suspected him.'

'I'm going back to the house to change into my other clothes and pick up my own shooting irons,' he announced to Soak.

The little man got up. 'You want I should come with you, Sam?'

Sam shook his head. 'No need. You might take a look around the saloons and sort of spread the word I'm the new sheriff.'

Soak nodded. 'Sort of start baitin' the trap,' he said. 'And it's my guess those rats will show themselves soon enough.'

Sam stayed in the house long enough to change. His first call was to the undertaker's office, where he made the final arrangements for Joel's funeral the following afternoon. Then, since it was not yet five, he decided he should visit Charles Cameron at the bank.

He found Virginia's father in his office, but the stout man gave him no friendly welcome. The puffed face of the banker showed anger as he noticed the badge Sam was wearing.

'What kind of nonsense is that?' he demanded, pointing to the star.

'It means I'm takin' over for Joel,' Sam said evenly.

This seemed further to infuriate the banker. The mean currant eyes in the fat folds of his face glittered with derision. 'What a fool idea that is,' he snapped. 'It seems to me you Wallaces have caused this town enough trouble. Why don't you do the decent thing and get out of Grant City pronto!'

'Not before I settle a few things.'

'Cause more trouble, you mean,' Charles Cameron snapped. 'Hard as it was for Virginia to go through what she did today, I'd say it was better for her than being married to your brother!'

It was Sam's turn to feel sudden fury. His hand reached down to touch the cold steel of his Colt, and he had trouble restraining himself from pistol-whipping the insolent banker.

'I reckon you don't mean that,' he said, his thin face white with rage.

Cameron was apparently unaware of the anger his words had inspired. 'You know I mean it,' he went on. 'Your brother was somehow mixed up in the rustling that's been going on, likely getting a cut from the gang for turning his back at the right time. Only today they decided to pay him off in lead instead of cash!'

Sam stared at the banker's sneering face. 'You're lucky Virginia is your daughter,' he said in a tense voice. 'And thank her that I don't make you pay here and now for what you said about Joel.'

At last the stout man recognized the dangerous mood Sam was in. He looked wary and said, 'I only wanted to give you some good advice, let you know folks here won't welcome you taking over as sheriff. They'll figure you're trying to cover up for Joel or cut in on the graft he was getting for himself.'

Sam shook his head disgustedly. 'I honestly didn't think you were this rotten! You can say things like that, with Joel lying dead down the street in the funeral parlor!'

Charles Cameron scowled down at his desk top. 'Better to get things straight than to indulge in a lot of pious talk.'

'I'm not interested in your moral opinions,' Sam said with deep sarcasm. 'I would like to know how Virginia is and whether or not she'll be able to attend the funeral tomorrow.'

The currant eyes raised to meet his. 'Virginia is terribly upset,' her father announced. 'I have sent her to Arvilla to stay with her aunt for a few weeks.'

The news left Sam both relieved and saddened.

'Maybe it's the best idea,' he said.

'Naturally,' her father snapped.

Sam had one more item to settle before taking his leave of the banker. Fixing his eyes on the stout man, he said, 'You and Joel had an argument over that anonymous message sent you, saying Joel was mixed up in the rustling. I think it might be an important clue. I'd like to have it so I could try and trace it to the sender.'

Cameron was instantly on his guard. 'I don't have it!'

'What do you mean?' Sam asked, at once suspicious of his reaction.

The stout man waved a pudgy hand. 'It's as simple as that. I don't have it. I left it with your brother.'

Sam knew this was a lie. He had been there during the argument and seen the note in the banker's hand. He couldn't actually remember, but he was almost certain Cameron had put it back in his pocket. Certainly he hadn't given it to Joel.

He said, 'I was there. I don't remember Joel getting the note.'

'I can't help that,' Cameron said irritably. 'I gave it to him just the same.'

Once again Sam saw that he was up against a blank wall. Charles Cameron was a shrewd customer who could lie and bluff as well as the next one. The banker was not going to give him any help if he could avoid it. He'd have to let the business of the note drop until a later time.

He said, 'When you see Virginia, tell her I was asking for her.'

Cameron eyed him coldly. 'I don't expect to be seeing her for a few days at least.'

Sam noted that the banker had made no promise to convey his message, and this didn't surprise him. As things stood now, Cameron and he were enemies. When the time came, he would seek out Virginia himself if he had anything to tell her. With this thought in mind, he gave the banker a nod and strode out of the office. He was still seething with rage when he reached the wooden sidewalk.

He walked slowly toward the center of town, a frown in his handsome face, and so occupied with his thoughts that he was oblivious to the people he passed.

All at once he realized that he'd eaten nothing since early morning. Now he felt weak and slightly nauseated without actually being hungry. Yet he knew he should force himself to eat.

Laura Thorpe's Grant City Saloon offered a sumptuous free buffet to the patrons of the saloon. Coffee was also available there, and so he decided to cross the street and make his first appearance in a public place since the murder.

Fortunately, there was no one whom he knew loitering outside the saloon entrance, and those that were standing there didn't seem to recognize him or notice the sheriff's star he was wearing. Inside, the big room was not as brightly lighted as it would be for the evening trade. It was also curiously silent and empty of all but a few drinkers lined up at the bar. Sam went directly to the free lunch and, taking a plate, helped himself generously to slices of roast beef, bread, pickles, and finally got some coffee from the bartender.

His hands full, he made his way to a table in the rear and sat down. As he had feared, his stomach rebelled when it came to the actual business of eating. Taking a lot of time, he forced some of the food down bite by bite and help it on its way with copious drinks of the steaming coffee. He had finished all he could and was lighting a cigarette when Laura Thorpe appeared.

The lovely redhead seemed startled to find him there. She sat down beside him, saying, 'This is the last place I expected to see you.'

He shrugged. 'In time of trouble, we turn to our friends. Aren't you my friend?'

She touched his arm. 'Of course, Sam! You can always count on me! I still can't accept what happened this morning. I go over it in my head and tell myself it was a nightmare, something I had a bad dream about!'

‘A bad dream we all shared,’ he said soberly.

Now her eyes fell on the badge, and something close to consternation crossed her pretty face. ‘Sam, have you gone clean crazy?’

‘Why?’

‘That badge. You’re not serious! You’re not going to follow Joel as sheriff?’

‘Doesn’t that make sense to you?’ he asked. ‘It does to me. I want to settle with Joel’s killers, and this way I can do it legal.’

Laura leaned close to him. ‘Get yourself drilled full of holes legal, just like Joel did,’ she warned him in a low voice. ‘I told you there is bad trouble brewing in this town. Don’t be a fool and mix in it.’

He flicked the ash from his cigarette and regarded her soberly. ‘You’re telling me to run out on Joel?’

‘No one can help Joel now,’ she said quickly. ‘I’m advising you to leave this town for good. Forget about the shooting, forget about being sheriff, forget there ever was a Grant City!’

His blue eyes met hers. ‘Forget about you, too?’ he asked quietly.

Her pretty face shadowed, and the corners of her mouth drooped. ‘Yes,’ she said in a low voice. ‘Forget me as well, since it can mean your life.’

He was going to make an answer to this when his attention was caught by a couple of newcomers who had pushed their way through the swinging doors and were heading for the bar. It took only a glance to see that one of the men was Ben Halliday, the burly son of the owner of the Circle 3 Ranch. And Halliday had spotted him, for now the big man, a leering expression on his face, changed direction to come slowly toward the table where Sam was seated with Laura.

CHAPTER FOUR

Laura followed Sam's glance and was at once aware of the approach of the hulking young man. She turned to Sam again with a warning look, but he was already on his feet, his hands reaching for his Colts and his eyes fixed on Ben Halliday.

A nasty grin crossed the face of the ranch owner's son as he paused a few feet from the table. 'So Grant City has a new sheriff!' he said derisively.

'Any objections?'

'Maybe you'll give up the job as quick as your brother did,' Ben said. 'And maybe you'll do it the same way.'

'I don't know just what you're hinting,' Sam said. 'But I don't like the tone of it.'

Ben shrugged. 'Then I don't blame you for latching onto a good thing. Only I warn you to keep your thieving hands off the Circle 3 stock from now on!'

Laura frowned at the overgrown youth. 'There's no call for that kind of talk, Ben Halliday,' she said. 'Sam has taken over as sheriff to bring us law and order, and I reckon he'll do a good enough job if we give him proper support.'

'Law and order!' Ben scoffed. 'The same kind his brother brought us. He and that rustling gang bled the Circle 3 white.'

Sam had heard as much as he could stand. Very slowly he circled around the table to come face to face with the blustering Ben. 'You spill a heap of loose talk for somebody that's never counted for much except being his father's son,' he told Ben. 'From now on I don't want to hear you mention Joel's name!'

Ben Halliday glared at him. 'You're talking big,' he sneered, 'because you've got the protection of that tin star. This is something that should be settled with fists.'

Sam gave a quick glance around the nearly empty saloon and decided this might be the moment to have a showdown with the arrogant Ben. He gave the frightened Laura a quick side glance. 'I'll try not to mess things up too much,' he told her. And at the same time he unbuckled his gun belt and tossed it on the table. Then very calmly he removed his sheriff's star and dropped it beside his weapons. Turning to Ben again, he said, 'All right, Ben! Let's do it your way, settle it man to man!'

Ben gave an uneasy look in the direction of the older man who had come in with him. He said, 'Make sure there's fair play, Buck!' And removing his gun belt, he tossed it to his henchman and then gave him his Stetson. An ugly grin crossed the young man's face as he crouched, ready to mix it with Sam. Sam regarded him coldly. He knew what Ben must be thinking. The young man was a lot heavier than he was; those fists would pack a murderous punch. Also, Ben had age on his side.

Sam moved in slightly, knowing this would be no Sunday school picnic. He let the burly youth come close without making any show of resistance. It was part of his plan to put Ben off-guard, make him careless. Then, with a quick movement, Sam punched his opponent hard just below the ribs. Ben gave a gasp of surprise and tumbled back. Sam pressed close to him and drove some additional body blows with both hands.

Now Ben rallied to attack and landed a heavy right to Sam's jaw that sent him reeling. The burly youth seemed not to have suffered from the punishment he'd taken so far. He rushed at Sam again, but this time Sam sidestepped and drove for Ben's mouth. He caught the young man squarely with a blow so hard it fairly lifted him free of the ground for a second and sent him staggering back. There was a roar of excitement from the crowd that had suddenly gathered in the previously empty saloon. It took no time for word of a fight to spread in the cow town, and now there was a full circle of onlookers around the battling men.

Ben was on one knee, with blood pouring from his mouth. He shook his head angrily and spat out what could have been a tooth. Sam waited, slightly crouched, wary of what his opponent might do next.

All of a sudden Ben rushed at him and grabbed him around the knees in a surprise movement that caught Sam off-guard. The big man slammed him heavily to the floor. And Ben was on his feet, lashing at Sam with his spurred boots. With a rolling motion Sam got to his feet again.

Ben met him with a fist that had the weight of a mule, and Sam felt his own mouth ripped open. The blow sent him staggering against a spectator, who rudely shoved him back into the ring.

The crowd let out another roar of encouragement as Ben came after him. The ranch owner's son flailed at him wildly, and some of the blows hit home and hurt. Ben's face was a puffed, bloody mess, and an eye was closing, but Sam knew he couldn't be much better off. He feinted, falling away, then moved in and caught his opponent squarely on the jaw again. There was a sickening smack and Ben looked startled and glassy-eyed, but recovered in a second to catch Sam in the body.

Now Sam made a supreme effort and, with all the boxing skill at his command, pummeled the ranch owner's son about the face and chest. The barrage of blows gave Sam the advantage, and Ben seemed too startled to fight back as he accepted the punishment.

He crouched very low, with a murderous expression on his badly swollen face, and suddenly made a swift gesture that put Sam on his guard. Ben's right hand had reached for his shirt front, and a second later he saw the gleam of the knife blade in his opponent's hand. Laura Thorpe cried out a shrill warning over the murmurs of the crowd surrounding them.

Sam dived at the man with the knife, giving Ben no chance to lunge at him first. He punched a right to Ben's mouth, that was now a soggy, blood-smeared pulp. Then he grabbed his shoulder and wheeled him around, at the same time snatching the hand with the knife and jerking it high as he rammed his knee directly in the small of the big man's back.

'Let go!' he warned him.

Ben's answer was an oath. So Sam let the knee slam hard against his opponent's ribs and spine. Ben cried out in pain and let the knife clatter to the floor. Sam relaxed his terrible grip on the big man, only to see he had made a mistake. With a roar of triumph, Ben broke loose and dived for the weapon. Sam caught the big man's face with his knee, and it sent him tumbling back on the floor. He followed his advantage by leaping on the prostrate young bully, a foot on Ben's right hand. There was a crunch of flesh and bones as the hand was crushed under the harsh impact. Sam stepped back, breathing heavily, and stood staring at the young giant writhing on the floor and groaning piteously.

The assembled spectators let out a roar of delight, and then Laura Thorpe burst through the crowd to come over and urgently tug on his arm.

'Come with me,' she said in a voice filled with authority.

He followed the saloon owner, picking up his gun belt and star as he went by the table at which he'd been sitting when Ben first arrived.

It was quiet in Laura's private office, and he sat in one of the plain chairs while she worked on his injured face with a cloth and cold water.

'You're making every mistake in the book,' she declared bitterly. 'The first one was taking that star. And the second one was roughing it up with young Ben Halliday.'

Sam winced slightly as she dabbed at a deep cut at the corner of his mouth. 'He had to be shut up,' he said.

'And you think you did it?'

'He's not likely to come throwing his weight around me any longer,' Sam said.

'That won't end it,' Laura warned him, standing back to survey him wearily. 'Just a couple more blows from those mule fists of Ben's, and you wouldn't be beautiful any more,' she told him.

He managed a rueful smile. 'Good looks aren't vital to a sheriff, are they?'

'You've got no right to that nice face,' she said, teasing him. 'You don't know how to take care of it.'

Sam touched a hand to his jaw and felt it gingerly. 'As long as I'm able to chew my food tomorrow, I'll be satisfied.'

Laura fixed a plaster on a cut above his eye. 'There,' she said. 'That's all I can do for you.'

He got to his feet and smiled. 'I'm mighty grateful,' he said. 'I didn't expect to have my own private nurse.'

'Don't count on it if you get in trouble again,' she warned him. 'And please don't start any more of your shenanigans in my saloon. Let the Longhorn have the option of your battles.'

Sam said, 'You may be making a mistake. We drew quite a crowd into the place just now.'

Laura was wearing a blue dress in a pale shade that suited her complexion. It occurred to him that she was still as much of a beauty as she'd been before she was married and widowed. Indignation had brought a dab of color to her cheeks and underlined her pert loveliness. The soft green eyes of the girl studied him fondly.

'You're the one making the mistake,' she said. 'Don't you realize what's going on here? Joel is laid out in his coffin just down the street because he got in someone's way. Why do you have to make yourself the next candidate for a cut-rate funeral on the town?'

'You know how I felt about Joel. I can't leave without squaring things for him.'

'Sentimental guff!' she snorted. 'You hadn't seen him for two years!'

'He was my brother!'

'You don't have to tell me that,' she said. 'But brothers can be as far apart as strangers. Do you think you really knew the kind of man Joel had become? Can you be certain he was as innocent of involvement with the rustling gang as you want to believe? You've changed since you left here. Even I can see that. Didn't Joel beat your time with Virginia? Were you happy that he won your sweetheart while you were away?'

His face clouded. 'None of that matters now.'

Laura flashed a knowing feminine smile. 'I

was sure you were still in love with her. You like the innocent little hazel-eyed ones, don't you, Sam?'

It was Sam's turn to feel his own cheeks crimson. He said, 'I'd appreciate it if you left Virginia out of this.'

'Too pure for me even to talk about,' Laura taunted him.

'That's not the point at all,' he protested.

The green eyes flashed angrily now.

'You know what you've started I hope,' she said. 'What will happen next? The Hallidays will go after you. When old Jim sees Ben and what you did to his gun hand, there's going to be some royal wrath at the Circle 3.'

'Jim Halliday may be king of this cow country,' Sam said, 'but his son and heir to the throne is not going around using knives to settle his battles while I'm sheriff.'

'You may not be sheriff long when the Hallidays get through with you,' she said. 'They'll fight you through the town council and beyond. I know them.'

Sam moved toward the door, then turned to say, 'It seems to me you don't have much confidence in me.'

'You were lucky enough to get away from here,' she said. 'You should have stayed. It's too bad you had to come back, Sam. And it's still not too late to ride away from all the mess that is no concern of yours.'

'I wish I could,' he told her. 'I've never

been one to hanker after trouble. But there are times when a man just doesn't have any choice.'

'You always were stubborn, Sam!'

He nodded. 'I'll know where to come the next time I get beat up, anyway.'

She followed him to the door, an enigmatic expression on her pretty face. 'Better not count on me for that. Better not count on me for anything!'

It was the hour for the evening meal, and the streets of Grant City were relatively quiet. The crowd that had gathered in the saloon for the fight had vanished, and there were only a few stragglers standing on the wooden sidewalk. There was no sign of Ben Halliday or his companion, so Sam guessed they must have gone off somewhere.

Sam stood for a moment on the steps of the saloon and noticed one mustached cowpoke nudge his younger companion. Then both of them turned their backs on him. He knew he wasn't going to be too popular in Grant City. The day was still bright with the setting sun as he descended to the sidewalk and then proceeded to cross the broad rutted main street in the direction of Lean Jim Slade's Longhorn Saloon.

The saloon was busier than the Grant City had been, as the early evening crowd was beginning to gather at the bar. There was no one playing the piano yet, and only the sound of loud male voices and occasional raucous laughter filled the stale, smoke-ridden air of the big saloon.

Then he saw Lean Jim Slade standing at the bar in conversation with a Mexican type. The gambler owner of the Longhorn was puffing on a rich-looking long cigar, and the moment he spotted Sam he moved away from the bar and came slowly forward to greet him. There was a thin smile on the gambler's gaunt face.

Removing the cigar from his mouth, he said, 'Seems as if you're already wearing the scars of office, Sheriff.'

'Just so long as I earned them in a good cause,' Sam said.

Lean Jim Slade nodded slyly. 'The word is that you did. I take it this is a get-acquainted call.'

'I wanted to let you know I was wearing the star in Grant City,' Sam said.

'I heard that some time ago,' Lean Jim Slade assured him. 'It seems fitting we should sit down to a drink.'

Sam hesitated and then decided it might be a good move, if he wanted the owner of the Longhorn to open up and spill some information. He said, 'I don't mind if I do. Double whiskey.'

After the gambler had ordered drinks and they had seated themselves at a table suitably remote from the bar, the elegantly dressed thin man gave him a knowing look as he raised his glass of cognac. 'To the success of our new sheriff.'

Sam studied his whiskey. 'I reckon I can't drink a toast to myself,' he said. 'I'll just say: To law and order in Grant City.'

'I'm all for that,' Lean Jim Slade said, sipping his cognac as Sam gulped down part of his double whiskey and felt better as the burning liquid went coursing down his gullet.

'You knew Joel pretty well?' Sam said, studying the gambler across the table.

'Yes, I did,' Lean Jim Slade said. 'I didn't like him, and he carried on a feud with me. We were natural enemies. I imagine you've been told that.'

'I have.'

The gambler's shrewd eyes fixed on him. 'Then it doesn't bother you?'

'Why should it?'

Lean Jim Slade smiled slowly. 'You sound like a sensible young man,' he said. 'It could be we might learn to live and let live; maybe even be friends.'

'Could be,' Sam said, and drained the rest of his whiskey.

The gambler paused a minute. 'One thing I'd like you to know,' he said. 'I didn't have anything to do with your brother's being shot down.'

Sam sat back in his chair. 'I'd expect you to say that, anyway.'

'I suppose so.' There was an edge in Lean Jim Slade's voice. 'But it also happens to be the truth.'

Sam remained completely motionless except for opening and closing his hands on the arms of the chair; his blue eyes searched the gambler's thin face.

He said, 'Then maybe you can tell me who did shoot Joel?'

The hollow-cheeked face of the gambler took on a wary expression. 'What makes you think that?'

'You're in a position to know a lot of what is going on.'

'True,' the other man said softly.

'I'd like to hear anything you know.'

Slade leaned back in his chair and touched the points of his slim fingers together as he eyed Sam speculatively. 'It doesn't always pay to talk,' he reminded him. 'Sometimes the consequences can be violent for the informer.'

'While I'm sheriff here, I can promise you protection,' Sam said.

'That sounds like a very interesting deal.' Slade smiled.

'I won't go along with anything crooked,' Sam warned him at once. 'But I'll make certain you don't suffer for helping me.'

The gambler delicately arched an eyebrow. 'Now you make it seem less interesting.'

'I'm playing fair with you.'

'I'll give you credit for that,' Slade agreed.

'I expected you'd hit the trail at once, looking for the killers.'

'What trail?' Sam asked. 'I don't have much to go on. I figured that I should turn up some information here in town first so I might have some idea who I was looking for.'

'I've heard talk one of the bandits looked a lot like Bull Bender,' the gambler said.

'That's no special information,' Sam retorted. 'I've heard that, too. Has Bender been in town lately?'

'Not in here,' Slade said. 'The place has been off limits to him ever since he started a row in here one night. My boys have orders not to serve him or any of his crowd.'

'But he has been in town?'

'Give me a little time,' Slade said. 'I'll ask some questions. Maybe I'll come up with an answer or two for you.'

Sam stood up. 'When?'

'Later,' the gambler said with a shrug. 'I'll have to see the right people. I can't actually give you a time.'

'I'll be back tomorrow night,' Sam said.

The gambler rose. 'Any time, Sheriff. You're always welcome. And by the way, I plan to attend your brother's funeral tomorrow. A mark of respect for an enemy, you might say.'

'Thanks,' Sam answered curtly. 'No doubt he would have been glad to do the same for you.' And with that he turned and headed for the door. He was conscious that the gambler was watching him out and not at all certain that Lean Jim Slade was as willing to help him as he pretended.

CHAPTER FIVE

There was no excitement the rest of the night. Sam Wallace made his rounds of the town and found most of the populace in a strangely subdued mood. Even in that hard-bitten frontier town, the morning's shooting had made an impact.

The lamp-lit stores and saloons were still open and doing business when he mounted his roan and left the main section of town for the isolated jail house. Deputy Wade Smith was seated at his desk in the swivel chair, his big head slumped forward on his chest as he snored noisily. On the sofa, Soak Dooley was also stretched out in a heavy sleep, and the stench of whiskey that emanated from the area of the sofa indicated that he must have fallen heir to some of his favorite medicine. Sam surveyed the two old men with a grim expression and then decided he would ride back to the house without bothering either of them.

He went out, swung into the saddle again and nudged the roan off in the direction of town once more. It was a dark night without any moon, and even after his eyes became accustomed to the shadows the visibility was extremely limited. He had arrived at the end of the main street and taken a side road that led to the street above where the homestead was located. It meant passing a number of old sheds that were used for storage by the town's hardware store.

Suddenly the roan showed signs of uneasiness. It gave a low whinny, and he leaned forward in the saddle to speak reassuringly to the spirited animal and stroke its soft mane. It was then he heard a rustle from the shacks on his left. Sitting very straight in the saddle, he reached for his Colt.

A shot flamed out in the darkness and whistled close to his head. At once he ducked and tried to rein the wildly rearing, frightened roan. He peered into the darkness surrounding the shacks and thought he made out the figure of a rider lurking there. He blazed away in that direction but could not tell whether he'd made a hit or not. As he still fought to control his own terrified horse, he was certain he heard the thud of hooves retreating back of the buildings. This would mean that whoever it was had beaten a retreat to the main street, where it would be almost impossible to pick him out from the other riders coming and going.

With the roan under control again, Sam

deliberately risked more danger by heading it across to the dark old buildings. He rode between them and in the rear of them, but there was nothing to be seen and only silence. Yet he knew that, moments before, someone had waited there to cut him down. At last he gave up the search and rode on to his home.

Sam made his way into the house and upstairs. When he finally slept, his dreams were haunted by strangely confused episodes of violence in which a grinning Bull Bender and Ben Halliday played major roles. He awoke feeling little refreshed.

The same faithful neighbor women who had been on hand to comfort his aunt the previous day had returned to look after the house until the funeral was over. They had his breakfast ready and waiting, although he ate only a little and that merely so their feelings wouldn't be hurt. Afterward he went up and spent a little time with Aunt Maggie.

The old woman, propped against her pillows, seemed to have grown perceptibly older and more feeble since the killing of her favorite nephew. Now she studied Sam with beseeching eyes.

'You mustn't wear that badge,' she pleaded. 'Not after what it brought Joel.'

He patted the old woman's thin hand with its soft brown-splotched skin. 'You needn't worry,' he said. 'It will be all right.'

'You're going to stay in Grant City?' she

said. 'You won't be leaving me?'

'I'll be staying,' he promised, not thinking it necessary to tell her at this time that his stay was bound to be short.

He went downstairs and, after exchanging a few words with the women about his aunt's general condition, went out to the barn to saddle the roan.

Within a quarter-hour he was tying it at the hitch post in front of the jail. Both Deputy Wade Smith and Soak Dooley were there and on the job. Soak came forward excitedly.

'Things are moving fast this morning,' he said.

'What do you mean?' Sam asked.

From his favorite seat in the swivel chair, Deputy Wade Smith supplied the answer with a look of grim satisfaction on his gray-mustached face. 'A messenger came here from the mayor a few minutes ago. He wants you to be at his office in town at ten o'clock sharp.'

Soak Dooley nodded. 'So that means something is doing. Maybe he knows now who did the shooting.'

'Maybe,' Sam said quietly, although privately he had an idea the summons had nothing to do with that. He asked Deputy Wade Smith, 'Any new customers last night?'

'Just a drunk who smashed a window in the hardware store,' the old man said. 'He's still sobering up.'

Standing in the center of the room between his two deputies, Sam frowned. 'Someone tried to take a pot shot at me last night,' he revealed to them.

Soak Dooley's lined purple face showed angry astonishment. 'Now I call that too much of a good thing! They weren't satisfied with getting poor Joel; they had to try for you as well!'

Deputy Wade Smith ran a hand nervously through his straggly gray mustache. 'Just when did this happen?'

'I came by here,' Sam said. 'You two were both asleep, and everything was quiet, so I decided to go home. It was on the way I heard someone off in the darkness, in that side street that leads up to my place. Someone was hiding among the shacks there.'

'Get any kind of a look at them?' Soak wanted to know.

He shook his head. 'I fired into the darkness, but I didn't expect to have any luck. Then I heard whoever it was riding away.'

Deputy Wade Smith looked grim. 'This ain't a very healthy spot for the law just now.'

'Especially if your name happens to be Wallace,' Sam agreed.

'If you're goin' to stay on here, you got to be more careful,' Soak told him. 'You shouldn't go anywhere after dark without one of us.'

'It would have happened just the same,' Sam said. 'And that bullet might have connected with whoever was along.'

'The best way to end all this is to catch up with whoever is responsible for the rustling,' was Deputy Wade Smith's comment. 'And that ain't goin' to be an easy job.'

Sam strolled slowly over to the window and stared out at the hitching post and the road beyond for a moment. Then he turned back to the other men, saying, 'I've been thinking about the rustling. From what I understand, most of the stolen cattle wind up on the Chisholm Trail and are sold in Abilene stockyards.'

'That's the story,' Deputy Wade Smith said.

'They are sold under the brand of the Cactus 8, and it's generally agreed the brands have been changed from the Circle 3 or some other easily switched brand.'

'There sure ain't no Cactus 8 ranch we've been able to locate,' Soak Dooley said. 'Joel spent a heap of time making sure of that. Yet cattle showing the C8 brand keep turning up in the Abilene market.'

Sam said, 'Since the dealers have been alerted, why do they keep on buying stolen stock?'

Deputy Wade Smith shrugged. 'Because somebody offers them the cattle at a low price. There's plenty of competition for good beef on the hoof, and always somebody ready to make a deal, whether it's on the level or not.'

'How about the law in Abilene?' Sam asked. 'Can we get any cooperation from that end?'

Soak shook his head. 'Don't count on it, Sam. When Wild Bill Hickock was marshal of Abilene, he kept in touch with Joel. As soon as he left to tour the East with Buffalo Bill, we never had any more reports.' The little man looked at Deputy Wade Smith for confirmation, asking, 'You notice any change?'

'No,' the old man said. 'Joel was complaining about it just a few days back. I think whatever is to be done has to be done right here.'

'I was afraid of that,' Sam said, 'but I thought I should at least find out what the chances were.' He moved to the door. 'I'd better get along to the mayor's office and see what's in store for me.'

Soak followed him. 'You want me to come along?' he asked.

Sam shook his head. 'No. That won't be necessary.' He eyed the heavy stubble of gray beard on the deputy's face. 'You better shave off some of that cactus if you're going to stay on as my deputy. And besides, there is the funeral this afternoon.'

The little man looked guilty and ran a hand

across his chin. 'Sure, Sam. I plumb forgot. I'll borrow a razor from Wade here and have myself respectable before you get back!'

Sam nodded and went out.

The mayor's office was located between the hardware store and the Longhorn Saloon. It was a new building but not a large one, and from it Steve Randall conducted his law business and also took care of his duties as the elected head of Grant City. When Sam rode up, he noticed there were several other horses tied to the hitching post. It looked as if the mayor had some other visitors.

He went into the outer office and told a pinched, middle-aged clerk who he was and that the mayor had requested that he come by. The clerk, who had an unpleasant squint, eyed him suspiciously and then went out back through a wooden door to an inner office. After a moment he returned to show Sam in.

Mayor Steve Randall got up from behind his desk at once. 'You're right on time, Sam,' he said. And with a gesture, 'I reckon you know everyone here.'

Seated in the room were three other men. One he recognized at once as James Halliday, the owner of the Circle 3 and Ben's father. Beside him was the older man who'd been with Ben when the fight began. The last person to catch Sam's attention was Jack O'Rorke, a slender man in his thirties who, he recalled, was prominent among the new landowners and farmers and often acted as their spokesman.

Sam nodded. 'Sure; I know everyone here,' hc said.

The mayor indicated an empty chair. 'Then make yourself comfortable,' he said, 'and we'll get down to business.'

James Halliday's bearing was as arrogant as that of his son, though concealed by a show of dignity befitting an older man. His handsome face was flushed with anger as he turned to Sam and said, 'First, I'd like to make a complaint.'

'About what, sir?' Sam asked, knowing only too well what the charge would be.

'About what you did to my son Ben,' Halliday said angrily. He glanced at the mayor. 'Do you know that because of what this new sheriff of yours did, my boy will likely wind up with a permanently crippled right hand?'

Mayor Steve Randall raised his eyebrows. 'What about it, Sam?'

'I had to break his hand because he was trying to use a knife on me!' Sam told the mayor in a quiet voice.

'That's a monstrous lie!' Big James Halliday roared.

'I can produce maybe fifty witnesses who saw what went on,' Sam said.

The big man pointed to the older cowpoke who had been with his son. 'And I've got one right here who will tell you that Ben had no intention of using that knife. Sure; he carried one on him as a last resort weapon. A lot of us do in this outlaw country. But he didn't reach for it. It fell out of his shirt, and right off you stamped on him like he was some kind of rat!'

'Those are not the true facts,' Sam said.

'Ask him!' James Halliday pointed to the cowpoke, who was hunched uneasily in his chair.

Mayor Steve Randall took the initiative. 'Is that the way you saw it?' he asked Halliday's unhappy witness.

'Sure,' the cowpoke said, averting his eyes from Sam. 'Sure. That's the way it went.'

Sam knew there was no use starting an argument on this point there and now. Later he'd rustle up witnesses of his own. He contented himself with directing a question at the cowpoke.

'Who started the fight in the first place?' he asked.

The cowpoke licked his lips. Then, with his eyes on the floor, he said, 'I can't rightly say. Ben went over to you, and you talked a bit. After that, the next thing I knew, Ben had taken off his gun belt and Stetson and was handing them to me.'

'I think you heard what was said,' Sam argued. 'And you know well enough it was Ben who began the trouble.'

James Halliday scowled at him. 'That

doesn't make it any easier to accept your brutality. I say a man like you isn't fit to wear that star.'

Now Jack O'Rorke spoke up for the first time. In his mild-mannered way he remonstrated with the ranch owner. 'That's a pretty strong statement, Jim. And it's not all that easy to find a man willing to take over as sheriff. Likely what happened was an accident. The sheriff was just trying to protect himself.'

'There wasn't any time to think of other ways of stopping him,' Sam said. 'I did what seemed best at the moment.'

Jack O'Rorke offered Sam an understanding smile. 'I can believe that, Sheriff. And we must also take into consideration another thing, gentlemen. This took place only hours after this man's brother was killed. I don't think it unnatural that his behavior should reflect the strain of what he'd undergone.'

'What it comes down to,' Jim Halliday rumbled, 'is whether you want to accept the word of this man or that of my son and his friend. I say he should be put out of office.'

'That hardly seems fair,' Jack O'Rorke said mildly. 'He hasn't been sheriff twenty-four hours yet. I say to give him a proper chance.'

Mayor Steve Randall, caught between the two opposing factions, cleared his throat and addressed himself to Jim Halliday. 'I dare say there are still facts to be revealed on both sides,' he said. 'But I'm inclined to go along with O'Rorke's view. I think Sam Wallace deserves some consideration.'

Jim Halliday's big frame vibrated with rage. 'What about my son?'

'I'm sorry about what happened to him,' the mayor said. 'But you can't really blame the sheriff for protecting himself against what he thought was an attack with a knife.'

'The knife was in your son's hand before it fell to the floor,' Sam said. 'I can prove that if I have to.'

'I see,' the ranch owner said harshly, and stood up. 'It's evident you are all against me.'

The mayor lifted a placating hand. 'That's not true, Jim!'

'I know the way things have been going,' the big man raged on. He turned to glare at Sam. 'I reckon you'll be another one to deal with the way we dealt with your brother. It's common talk he sold out to the outlaws and paid for it yesterday.'

Sam jumped up. 'You can't prove that!'

'I can prove it by the cattle missing from the Circle 3!' the big man retorted angrily. 'Your brother never lifted a finger to halt the rustling!'

'You shouldn't say that, Jim,' the mayor protested weakly, but the ranch owner was paying no attention to him.

'I've heard the stories spread about Joel,'

Sam told Jim Halliday. 'And I figure they began with you. You started them because you'd been hurt bad by the rustlers and wanted to take it out on someone.' He paused. 'I warn you I don't want to hear anything like them again!'

Jim Halliday was more than six feet tall. He stood before Sam, towering over him by at least a couple of inches. 'Don't threaten me,' he warned. 'And don't think I've finished with you yet.' He nodded to the cowpoke. 'Come on, Buck!' And the two of them stalked out.

After they had gone, Sam turned to the mayor. 'It seems Jim Halliday thinks he's the only one entitled to threaten anyone in this town.'

Jack O'Rorke, who was also on his feet now, gave a deep sigh. 'You mustn't let him bother you, Sam,' he said. 'Jim does have a lot of problems, and I guess we can admit to ourselves that one of them is Ben.'

The mayor nodded. 'He has a reputation for getting into trouble.'

The farmers' representative picked up his hat. 'I've got to be going, but if there's anything I can do, just let me know.' He paused. 'And about Joel: all of us on the council know he was an honest man, and his murder yesterday a real loss.'

'Thanks,' Sam said, touched by O'Rorke's words.

The farmers' man nodded and turned to the mayor. 'Don't accept his resignation under any circumstances, Mayor.' And with a smile, he left them alone.

The mayor looked at Sam.

'What do you plan to do next?'

'I'll be taking to the trail as soon as the funeral is over,' Sam said grimly. 'I'm looking for an outlaw called Bull Bender and maybe a couple of his cronies. I have an idea they may be hanging out near that mine of Barney Wales'.'

'Be sure and take Soak with you,' the mayor warned. 'That is outlaw territory up there. And the story is that this Barney Wales has gone crazy.'

'I know.' He nodded. 'Maybe I made a mistake to wait this long. If I'd left yesterday, I would have missed having that scrap with Ben Halliday and might have caught up with those killers by now.'

'I think you did right to wait,' the mayor said, 'if only as a mark of respect for Joel. What about Virginia? Will she be attending the funeral?'

'No. Her father took her to an aunt's place out of town.'

'I see.' The mayor's pleasant face was shadowed. 'Perhaps it's for the best. It will take her a while to recover from yesterday. A dreadful moment! I'll never forget that spatter of blood across her dress!'

'I aim to talk with her later,' Sam said. 'It could be she might know something that would help. I imagine Joel talked a lot to her.'

'A good thought,' the mayor agreed. He paused. 'I suppose you realize you'll get no help from her father? He was one of those who turned against your brother in the past few weeks. In fact, I began to wonder if he mightn't try to cancel the wedding.'

'I know about Cameron,' Sam said briefly. He had no desire to confide in the mayor concerning the bitter argument the two men had had the night before the wedding. 'Is there anything else?'

'Nothing. I'll see you at the funeral, of course.'

Sam nodded. 'I guess Deputy Smith can take care of things in Grant City while I'm on the trail.'

The mayor grimaced. 'Try not to stay away too long,' he warned. 'Smith is old and not too energetic by nature.'

'I know,' Sam said.

When he left the mayor's office, he rode back to the jail and remained there until it was time to get ready for Joel's funeral. The lone drunk who had been the jail's only customer had paid his fine and gone on his way. So there was no reason they all couldn't attend the service in the small cemetery just behind the church.

'Don't hardly seem possible,' Deputy

Wade Smith said with a frown. 'Joel will be buried just a few hundred feet from where he was married yesterday.'

'The kind of thing that don't bear thinkin' about,' Soak Dooley agreed. He had shaved and managed to get rid of his beard with only a few cuts to serve as witness to his shaky hand. He looked much more respectable now, and there was no question as to his sorrow about Joel.

Sam added nothing to the comments of the other two.

The three waited until almost the last minute, then closed the jail and rode forlornly in the direction of the cemetery. By the time they arrived, most of the others had gotten there ahead of them. The venerable old minister was at the graveside with Bible in hand, waiting for a signal to begin the actual burial service.

As Sam walked over to the grave, he saw the mayor, Laura Thorpe, his Aunt Maggie, supported on either side by the neighbor women and Lean Jim Slade, who had come as he'd promised, along with Jack O'Rorke and countless others from the town. Even Charles Cameron had turned up, no doubt for appearances only, an ugly expression on his puffy face as he stood beside the mayor with bared head.

Sam took his place on the other side of the mayor. The minister looked around and then, clearing his throat, opened the Bible as he prepared to begin the service. But before he could start, there was the sound of a carriage approaching. As it drew near the small circle of mourners, it was apparent this was some last minute arrival come to pay his respects to Joel. Sam raised his eyes to see who it might be.

He happened to glance Charles Cameron's way and noticed a look of consternation on the banker's unpleasant face. Then, turning toward the carriage again, he saw the door open. An elderly woman got out, followed by a wan Virginia Cameron, dressed entirely in black and wearing a black bonnet with a veil. Realizing that she must have come against her father's wishes, Sam acted on impulse. He moved across to the two women and took Virginia's arm.

The lovely girl was swaying slightly; she looked up at him. 'Thank you, Sam,' she murmured. 'Thank you.'

He led her close to the grave and nodded to the minister to begin so the ordeal would be over quickly for her. The old man opened his Bible again and began to speak. During the brief service Sam raised his eyes to glance at Virginia's father and noticed the expression of rage on the stout man's face. At the same time he caught a glimpse of Laura Thorpe and was startled to see the expression on her lovely features as she stared at the pathetic figure of

Virginia. It was one of pure hatred!

CHAPTER SIX

The service came to an end, and the old minister went over to offer his personal sympathy to Virginia and Sam. When he left them to speak with Sam's Aunt Maggie, the young sheriff escorted the grieving girl back to her carriage. While her elderly woman escort stood by, Virginia turned to him before stepping inside.

'Don't mind Father,' she said quickly. 'He refused to let me come today. But I made the trip anyway.'

'I know how it is,' Sam consoled her. 'Don't worry.'

'I'll be in Arvilla for a while,' she told him. 'Come when you can.'

'Depend on it,' he promised, and then stood back as her father bustled up.

'What madness brought you here like this!' Charles Cameron spoke angrily to the stricken Virginia. 'I wanted to keep you from making a spectacle of yourself.'

'I intended to come from the beginning, Father,' she said with a sudden cool calmness that surprised both Sam and her father.

Charles Cameron looked around with an uneasy expression. 'Let us not discuss it here,' he said in an abrupt about-face, helping her into the waiting carriage, then helping her woman escort, and finally getting in himself and closing the door. The last glimpse Sam had of the party was of the banker's livid face through the door glass as the carriage was quickly driven away.

Then he turned to speak to some of his other friends, trying to seek out Laura Thorpe first. But he was startled to discover that she had somehow managed to get away. He felt hurt and upset, because he'd wanted to speak with her. Also, he had been puzzled at the hostility she'd shown toward Virginia during the service. Surely she couldn't go on holding a grudge against the poor young widow!

Now he was suddenly surrounded by friends. Afterwards he could neither recall their words nor the blur of faces. He was grateful and thanked them. As soon as he decently could, he went to the grave for a last goodbye to Joel, after which he rejoined Soak Dooley and Deputy Wade Smith.

When they arrived back at the jail, he instructed Soak to pack provisions for several days on the trail. This provoked consternation in both of his deputies.

Soak studied him with wide eyes. 'You aim to be gone that long?'

'I'm ready to go alone,' Sam advised him. 'There's no need of your coming along.'

'That ain't what I'm worryin' about,' Soak argued. 'I just don't like the idea of spending all that time in outlaw country.'

'And what about the town?' Deputy Wade Smith demanded. 'Joel never called on me to do anything more than take care of the jail.'

'If you're planning to remain a lawman, you had better start acting like one,' Sam told the old man sternly. 'You have no prisoners here, so there is nothing to stop you from riding into town tonight and showing yourself in the saloons.'

Deputy Wade Smith tugged at his gray mustache furiously. 'Why, that would be just asking for trouble, Sheriff. Those toughs in town would like nothin' better than to make a fool of me.'

'You let them know you're wearing a law badge and stand for authority,' Sam said. 'And you can tell them for me they'll have me to deal with if something goes on while I'm away.'

The old deputy collapsed in his comfortable swivel chair. 'I don't like it,' he worried. 'I don't like it at all.'

Soak Dooley finally came in, looking tired and dejected. 'I got enough stuff loaded now,' he said. 'It's gettin' late. Wouldn't it be better to wait and make an early start in the morning?'

Sam shook his head. 'No. I've waited too long as it is. We'll leave now.'

It turned out there was to be another delay. He had no more than mounted the roan when he discovered it had a loose shoe. Getting down, he stroked the chestnut and white horse and examined its left rear hoof.

'No use starting out with that, fella,' he said gently. 'We'll have to go in town to the livery stable and get you properly shod.'

So he and a grumbling Soak Dooley rode back into town to the stable in the rear of the hotel. It was a busy place, and there were plenty of cowpokes standing around the yard and in the doorway. The stable itself was a big one, with its own blacksmith shop near the entrance. The flames from the forge could be seen from the yard.

Sam rode right up to the door and explained his problem to one of the stable boys, who at once led the roan inside so the blacksmith could take care of the faulty shoe. Meanwhile Soak Dooley was watering his sway-backed nag at the long water trough that occupied a prominent spot in the big yard.

Sam stood in the door of the stable for a few minutes while he took out the makings and rolled himself a cigarette. After he had lit it and had taken a few puffs, he strolled out to join Soak, who was engaged in a spirited conversation with a gray-bearded old-timer.

A burst of jeering laughter to his left caused him to glance that way, and he at once recognized the older cowhand whom Ben

Halliday had called Buck, and who had come to the mayor's office only that morning with big Jim Halliday to place charges against him. Buck was surrounded by a group of younger men who Sam decided must be hands from the Circle 3.

Ignoring the group, he continued on across the yard. Just as he was going past the watering trough, he heard quick footsteps coming up behind him, and a moment later he was roughly pushed from behind so that he staggered back against the horse trough and almost tumbled into it. As he recovered his balance, his arm was wet above the elbow. He turned angrily to see a tall young cowpoke grinning at him maliciously.

'Sorry, Sheriff,' the youth said in what was plainly a mock apology. 'I reckon I just didn't see you.' As he finished speaking, a roar of laughter went up from Buck and his cronies in the background.

Sam offered the tall cowpoke a slow smile. 'Sure,' he said. 'I understand. We all get sort of careless at times.'

And then, catching the other man completely off-guard, he grabbed him roughly around the throat and waist and tumbled him over into the trough. The tall cowpoke didn't know what was happening to him until he was angrily splashing in the shallow water. A silence fell over the others in the yard as the onlookers waited to see what would happen.

With a howl of rage, the rangy youth bounced out of the trough and reached for his gun. But Sam was already standing waiting for him with a grim smile and his Colt drawn.

'I may be careless,' he told the tall youth. 'But I'm a sure shot. I wouldn't try anything if I were you.'

The other man stood motionless, glaring at him for a few seconds. Then, with a shrug, he retrieved his hat from the ground and, dripping from his immersion, went back to join the others. Sam glanced after him and then returned his Colt to its holster as he went over to Soak Dooley and his old-timer friend.

Soak was grinning from ear to ear. 'That was a mighty fast bit of work, Sheriff,' he said. 'That fella needed to be cooled off some!'

The old-timer added his word of praise. 'I ain't seen anything like that around here for a long while.' He shook his head in disgust. 'Times ain't been the same since the buffalo herds were destroyed. All we got around here now are a lot of farmers!'

'Reckon the sheepmen will be moving in soon,' Soak agreed in the same tone. 'Then the country will be plumb ruined.'

Sam asked the old-timer, 'How long has Jim Halliday had his set-up?'

'Mebbe ten years,' the graybeard said, 'or a little longer. Jim was one of the first to bring cattle in. Now they've spread all over the grasslands. Jim is land greedy. He'd like to squeeze the rest of us out.'

Sam knew this was a familiar complaint among the small landowners. The big operators like Jim Halliday were always wanting to spread out, and they weren't too particular about how they got extra acreage.

'Understand you gave young Ben Halliday a nasty beating,' the old-timer said with a chuckle. 'I'd like to have been there when it happened. That youngster has gotten too big for his breeches!'

He paid little attention to the comment, for he saw the stable boy leading out the roan and knew it was ready for the road. Not only was he eager to get away from the tense atmosphere of the stable yard, but it was now growing late in the day, and there was no chance of getting to the hill country and Barney Wales' mine unless they got going at once.

'We can leave now,' he told Soak, and went over to get the roan and pay for the work done.

In the saddle, he noted that Buck and his crowd from the Circle 3 were standing back watching him with ugly expressions on their faces. He felt a lot easier when he and Soak were on the main street again and heading for the trail that led to the hills. The main heat of the day was over, and that would be in their favor. But he soon discovered Soak's estimate of the trail had been correct. It was rough, and a good deal of it was uphill. He kept the roan moving at a good pace, but he had to make allowances for Soak and his heavily loaded mount. Gradually the light faded, and by the time they had reached the country of tall evergreens and steep rocky slopes, daylight was almost gone.

Sam reined his mount at the crest of a winding trail that ended in a small plateau. He waited for the lagging Soak to catch up. When the little man at last reached him, he asked, 'How much farther is it to Wales' cabin and the mine?'

Soak's purple face frowned in concentration, and he lifted his hat to scratch his head. 'Shouldn't take us more than thirty minutes,' was his decision.

Sam looked around. It was grim, desolate country. 'It will be dark by then.'

'Knew that when we started,' Soak retorted.

As they rode on, the sun dipped and the shadows lengthened. The trail led through a pine thicket, and there it was almost dark. When they emerged at last to open land, it was barren and rocky. Soon Sam was barely able to make out Soak and his horse when he glanced back in the shadows.

The little man finally came riding close to him. 'We're there now,' he said. 'The cabin must be right ahead.'

Sure enough, they came to a clearing flanked on all sides by tall pines. When they rode up to the cabin, it was in darkness and there was no sign of life. They got off the horses and went to the door of the square log building. It was wide open, and inside Sam smelled the stale odor of fried food.

He turned to Soak. 'He can't be far away. Somebody has been cooking here lately.'

The little man nodded. 'Maybe if we could find a light—' he said.

After some searching, Soak came up with a lantern. In a moment they had it lighted and were viewing the interior of the log cabin by its wavering glow. The cabin was a mess. A table of dirty dishes and a stove covered with pots and pans abandoned without being cleaned were responsible for the stale stench of food. An unmade cot in a corner added to the general squalor. The bare floor was littered with cigarette butts, and there was a pile of broken glass by the stove as if someone had thrown a bottle against it, smashed it into bits and left the pieces there.

Soak's wizened face registered disgust. Taking it all in, he said, 'I thought my own place was bad, but this sure beats it.'

Sam was busy studying the details. 'Seems to me he must have had company lately, or else he's let his dishes and cigarette butts pile up a powerful long time.'

'And that's the truth!' the little deputy snorted.

Sam glanced at him. 'Where do you think we might find him?'

'Anywhere. Back in Grant City, maybe. He goes in there every so often.'

'Wouldn't we have met him on the trail?'

'There is more than one way up and down from this place,' Soak informed him.

Right then a sound came that made them both stand rigid with shock. It came from outside, some distance away: a weird kind of high-pitched laughter that had nothing human about it. It was loud, and when the dead silence of the isolated place took over again they exchanged startled glances.

'That weren't no animal,' Soak said, his face wearing a drawn look. 'And it didn't sound much like a human should.'

'Barney Wales?' Sam questioned.

'Reckon so,' Soak agreed unhappily. 'He must have gone clean crazy, judgin' by that.'

Sam sighed. 'At least we know he's around.'

'It'll be another thing to find him and get him to talk,' Soak grumbled as he moved to the doorway and, still holding the lantern aloft, peered out.

'See any sign of him?' Sam asked as he brushed by the little man and went out into the cold night air again. The horses pawed the ground restlessly, and one of them whinnied softly. There was no other sound to disturb the eerie quiet.

'The mine is over yonder,' Soak said from the doorway behind him. 'We could try it.'

'Yes,' Sam agreed. Then, gazing into the darkness, he called out, 'Barney Wales! We want to talk with you! Joel's been killed! We need your help!'

The words echoed mockingly in the clearing. He waited for an answer, hoping his message might have penetrated the befogged mind of the madman who was lurking somewhere in the shadows of the great pines. But no reply came; only that frightening silence again.

'He won't pay no attention,' Soak said, coming out carrying the lantern.

'So it seems,' Sam said.

'The entrance to the mine is about a hundred yards from here,' Soak told him. 'You want to take a look?'

'Yes. Lead the way.'

The little man went ahead, picking a path across the uneven surface of the open field. Sam followed, a grim expression on his thin face.

The field gave way to sloping chalky ground, and he followed Soak down a fairly steep incline to join him at an entrance to a tunnel about six feet wide and a few inches higher than his head.

'Ever been in here?' he asked Soak.

Soak's wizened features appeared in the lantern's light. 'Not since Wales has been working it,' he said. 'I was inside years back when a half-dozen from Grant City were operating the mine. Part of it joins with a natural underground cave. They gave up when the seam of ore played out. No one bothered about it afterward, at least not until Barney Wales decided there was still gold in the mine.'

'From what you say, we have less chance of locating him in there than we would outside,' Sam said. 'There must be plenty of hiding places for him.'

'No doubt about that.'

'Well, let's go,' Sam told the deputy impatiently. 'We can try, anyway.' He drew his Colt out of its holster and followed Soak with the gun ready. If the mine was serving as a hideout for the outlaws, he might have reason to use it.

The roof of the tunnel became lower once they were inside, and so they proceeded with their heads bent slightly. Sam noticed that the walls were dry and chalky, as was the surface overhead. The long passage seemed to stretch endlessly, and he began to wonder how air got into the place. Soak had spoken of it joining with a natural cave. Perhaps there were also passages that led to the open. Suddenly the little man halted and lifted a warning hand.

'Ahead!' he whispered for Sam's benefit.

Sam peered into the darkness and was at once aware of what had caught Soak's attention. The end of the tunnel was now lit by a rosy glow. And while he watched with fascinated eyes, a scarecrow figure stepped into view, holding a flaming torch over his head. It took only a moment for Sam to recognize Barney Wales. He was an emaciated, hollow-eyed ghost of the stalwart young man Sam had known, but there was enough resemblance to permit identification.

He pushed by Soak and ran down the tunnel until he was within thirty feet or so of the insane man. 'Barney,' he called out, 'it's Joel's brother, Sam! Joel's been murdered! We think you can help us find out who did it. We need to talk to you!'

'No!' the answer came in a croak from the throat of the weird, ragged creature who had once been Barney Wales.

'We mean you no harm!' Sam said, taking a few steps toward him.

The man holding the torch drew back. 'Don't come any closer!' he cried out in that odd, hoarse voice. 'It's all mine! You can't have any of it!'

'We're not after anything but information,' Sam told him.

Soak was at his elbow now. 'We just want to talk to you,' he called out to the maddened Wales. And then they both began to walk slowly toward him.

Wales' eyes darted madly from left to right. And then, with the scream of a cornered animal, he dashed off to the side as quickly as he had appeared. Sam at once raced after him, calling on Soak to follow. The little man lagged, and Sam had to depend on the sound of the madman's retreating footsteps to guide him. He braved the narrow darkness of the tunnel, which now began to twist and turn. Every so often his outstretched hands grazed against the tunnel sides, and he felt a burning pain as knuckles were scraped or cuts inflicted.

The glow of the torch had vanished, and he stumbled along in the darkness, no longer able to hear the madman's footsteps. He could hear Soak following along behind him.

Then, from shortly ahead, there came another wild animal scream; not laughter this time, but a cry that suggested sheer horror. It was followed by the sound of a great splash and another gasping shriek, then complete silence.

Sam raced on toward the sounds he had heard and turned a corner in the tunnel to come to a frantic halt. On the ground directly in front of him lay the still flaming torch. But the tunnel ended at that point, to give way to a great cavern with stalactites hanging eerily from above and, at a frightening distance below, an underground lake of still, murky water. Sam swayed on the edge of the precipice over which the insane Wales must have plunged to sink in those icy depths.

Soak came up to him and, taking in the situation, uttered a cry of alarm.

'He's a goner if he went down there,' the little man said, staring down at the sinister lake.

Only then did Sam realize he was trembling. 'I came near going right after him. I didn't know the tunnel ended here.'

Soak shook his head. 'Well, we won't be hearing anything from Wales.'

'Not now,' Sam agreed.

'Not likely he'd have been any help. He was a lot worse than the last time I seen him in the office.'

Sam stared down at the water. There was nothing to be done. He bent to retrieve the torch that Wales had left when he had made his death leap. At least he could make use of it on the way back. This time he took the lead. Soak had been right in saying there were several connecting passages in the old mine. They passed the openings to these, which he hadn't noticed earlier as he rushed along in the darkness. But there seemed no point in investigating the mine further now.

Gradually they drew closer to the mine entrance. Sam took a deep breath to fill his lungs with fresh air as he stepped out into the night. Then his whole body tensed as he heard a familiar sound: the thud of approaching horses. He raised the torch high and stared in the direction from which the sound came.

Soak ran out to join him. 'Someone coming!' he cried.

And as he uttered the words, the riders came into view. Too late Sam realized the torch and lantern made him and Soak Dooley easy targets. He was reaching for his Colt again when the men on the horses opened fire. As their guns blazed in the darkness, he caught a fleeting glimpse of the ugly face of Bull Bender. Then a searing pain shot through his head and he slumped down unconscious.

CHAPTER SEVEN

Sam was stretched flat on the gravel in front of the cave when he came to. Head spinning, he raised himself with a great effort and tried to collect his thoughts. There was a burning pain along the top of his skull, and, touching his fingers to his forehead, he felt a sticky wetness that was undoubtedly blood. The torch he'd been carrying had gone out when he fell. With a further effort he leaned on an elbow to turn around and see Soak Dooley in a crumpled heap behind him. The lantern was resting against a large rock at a drunken angle, but its wick still burned feebly to give off a little light.

Soak Dooley moaned and raised his head. 'Sam!' he called out weakly.

'Yes,' Sam answered. 'I'll be with you in just a minute!'

The little man's face was a study in pain. 'I been trying to get you to speak to me for a while now,' he said. 'I thought maybe you was dead.'

Sam touched his temple and said, 'They didn't do a good job. But I've got a ridge in my head that made me unconscious.' Ignoring his dizziness and pain, he staggered to his feet and went back to kneel beside the deputy.

Soak shook his head mournfully. 'They got me in the thigh. I been bleeding a lot, and I think the bone is shattered.'

He lifted the lantern up, held it close and was shocked by the pool of blood surrounding the little man's left leg. There was no doubt Soak had been badly hit.

Sam didn't want him to lose courage. He would need all his stamina before this ordeal was over. 'It's bad enough,' he acknowledged. 'But I think we'll be able to manage.'

Soak groaned. 'It's hurting fierce. I can't move, Sam.'

Sam's face was grim as he gave the leg a

brief examination. 'We'll have to improvise some bandages,' he said. 'Did you pack any whiskey for the trip?'

'Sure did!' the little man said. 'You'll find it in one of my saddle bags.'

'Good!' Sam said. 'We'll be able to use it.' And he began to untie his neckerchief to make an emergency bandage.

The little man got a good look at him in the lantern light and gasped. 'Sam,' he said, 'you're a sight to scare bears! Your face is a mess of blood!'

'I can believe that,' Sam said as he began gently to fix the neckerchief about the deputy's injured thigh.

Soak moaned as Sam disturbed the leg a little. He asked, 'Did you see who it was?'

'There were three of them,' Sam told him. 'And I recognized Bull Bender. There's not a doubt it was the same three who cut down Joel yesterday. I was hit before I had a chance to see the faces of the other two.'

'I didn't get a look at any of them,' Soak said, his voice tense with suffering. 'So it's the rustling gang after all. That means they must be holed up somewhere around here.'

'No question of that,' Sam agreed, as he finished his primitive first aid for the little man. 'They've been using the crazy man as a blind.'

The little man closed his eyes and gritted his teeth. 'They won't be able to do that any longer. Barney Wales is somewhere at the bottom of that lake, and I don't expect his body will ever be found.'

Sam stood up with the lantern in his hand. 'I've got to get you back to the cabin somehow.'

'I wish I could walk, Sam,' the little man said. 'But it's no use.'

'I can see that. I'll have to bring over your horse. Once I've helped you into the saddle, you should be able to get the short distance to the cabin.'

'I'll sure as heck try!'

'Wait here and don't worry,' Sam told him. 'I'll go for the horses. I don't think there is any danger of that crew returning.'

'Reckon they may not be far away,' Soak worried.

Sam stared down at the prone man. 'They sure enough made a mistake when they didn't fill us with lead instead of leaving us just half-dead.'

'Reckon they were in a hurry and counted on that crazy Wales to finish their job,' Soak said with a groan.

'I'll leave the lantern with you,' Sam said. 'You got your gun handy?'

'Right here,' Soak said miserably as he slowly lifted it up.

'You'll have it ready if anything does happen,' Sam said. 'I'll get back as quick as I can.'

'Will you be able to manage without a light?'

Sam nodded. 'I think it's the only way.' He didn't want to spell out that he was fearful the rustlers might be across the field in the log cabin. There was no light showing, but that didn't mean they weren't inside. This time he was not going to make an easy target of himself. With his Colt drawn, he began warily to start the return journey to the cabin in the enveloping darkness.

His step was unsteady and his head still light and hurting. But he had a shrewd suspicion his pain was by no means as severe as that of the deputy. The wound in Soak's leg was a bad one, and Sam knew that he had to get the little man to a doctor. The first step was to get him to the cabin. When morning came, he would have to figure out the rest.

As he approached the log cabin, Sam halted and listened intently. It was all quiet as before. But what had happened was a warning that the situation could alter rapidly. He was not anxious to walk into a trap. From a distance, in the rear of the cabin, he heard the nervous whinny of one of the horses. At least they were still there, he thought with relief. One of his worries had been that the outlaws might have taken them.

Now he moved on to the cabin and found it as empty as before. He made his way through the night to where the horses were tethered and prepared to ride back to Soak's aid.

The faint glow of the lantern served as a beacon for Sam's trip back to the injured man. Astride the roan and leading Soak's horse with its heavily laden pack saddles, he felt a little more in command of the situation. His head was still bothering him, and he hadn't done anything about the blood that had streaked down on his thin face. All that could wait until he'd gotten the deputy back to the cabin and made him comfortable.

Soak lifted his head and stared in his direction with a frightened look on his pinched face. Recognizing Sam as he dismounted, the fear gave way to relief. He lay back with a moan.

'I got the idea it was them back again,' he said. 'I could hear more than one horse.'

'I brought yours along,' Sam told him. 'We have to get you away from here.'

In the minutes that followed, he busied himself finding the whiskey and giving Soak a couple of stiff drinks from the bottle. He wound up taking a good swig himself, and once the potent liquor coursed through him he felt more equal to the problems facing him.

Soak also showed improvement as a result of his ration of whiskey. He even managed to grin wanly up at Sam and say, 'I may be hurting a lot worse than you, Sheriff, but I sure as shootin' don't look any worse.'

'Never mind about that,' Sam said. 'Do you think you can bear having me lift you up into the saddle?'

'What's got to be done has to be done,' was the little man's quiet acceptance of his plight.

It turned out to be a nasty, painful business. Once Soak's piteous moans almost made Sam give up. But he braced himself and blessed Soak for being a lightweight. At last he had him slumped in the saddle and began the short ride across to the cabin.

When they were there, it was a comparatively minor task to get the deputy over onto the cot. With the lantern on the table and them both safely inside for the night, he was able to clean himself up and apply better dressings to Soak's wound. He located the well outside the cabin and started a fire in the stove. Soon he had warm water and fresh bandages made from an extra shirt which he quickly tore into suitable strips. He washed his own face and gingerly cleaned up the slim ridge the bullet had traced on his skull.

Then he gave additional attention to Soak. It was again his impression that the leg wound the little man received was so serious it required the services of a doctor. Yet he did what he could to make him comfortable.

Soak stared up at the roof of the cabin with a grim expression. 'Sorry to be such a nuisance,' he said.

'You should blame me for getting you into this,' Sam told him.

The deputy winced as Sam daubed at the injured area with a warm cloth. 'Wales is settled, anyhow,' he said. 'He must have been plumb crazy to come up here in the first place. No one ever got anything out of that mine. The fellows that first worked it gave it up long ago. There may be lots of lead and zinc in Kansas, but there's precious little gold.'

Sam nodded. 'I'd say the only ones profiting from the mine were the rustlers. It made a good front for the operations they were carrying on. It wouldn't surprise me if they have a herd of stolen cattle hidden somewhere near here right now.'

'Must be something doing, or Bull Bender wouldn't be around.' The little man paused and looked at Sam with questioning eyes. 'Bender must have figured your brother was onto his game, and that's why he killed him, why he tried to do us in tonight.'

'Apparently,' he said, sitting back, his immediate work on the injured limb completed. 'But I doubt if Bender is the brains of the rustlers. My guess is there is somebody back of him who gives the orders. And that's the one who wanted Joel dead. That's who we have to connect with if we're to clear up the mystery.'

'It figures,' Soak agreed. 'You got any idea

who it might be?'

Sam shook his head. 'No. I only wish I had.'

It was a long night. Soak finally drifted into an uneasy slumber. Sam slept in a chair close to the deputy's bed. As morning drew near and a gray dawn streaked the sky, Soak came fully awake and seemed to be suffering a good deal. Sam was feeling far from well himself, but he went to work making coffee and a simple breakfast for them.

Soak managed some coffee but lay back with closed eyes when offered some bacon. 'I can't eat,' he moaned. 'Just let me be, Sheriff.'

Sam eyed him with concern. He had an idea the little man had a raging fever, and he knew that unless he got Soak back to town he would go rapidly downhill and probably die. He went outside and looked after the horses. At the same time he decided he would ride out and study the area around the mine.

He didn't have to ride far to find the valley with a small river running through it. Hidden from the rest of the country, it was an ideal spot to keep stolen cattle. He urged the roan down the steep grassy slope to the bottom of the valley and there found unmistakable signs that stock had recently been herded there. He scanned the hillsides for some sign of shacks, but there was none. This led him to the conclusion the rustlers must have made their headquarters at the mine's log cabin and merely kept their stolen cattle there. He would have liked to have stayed longer and made a more thorough investigation of the valley, but he was mindful of the injured man waiting for him back in the cabin, so he nudged the roan back up the sharp incline. He had confirmed his suspicions, even if he hadn't been able to bring Bull Bender in.

Now he had to cope with getting Soak back to Grant City. When he returned to the cabin, he was alarmed to find that the little man seemed worse. In desperation he fed him some more whiskey, and Soak showed some renewed interest in his plight.

'I've got to get you to the doctor in Grant City,' Sam told him.

Soak groaned. 'Maybe if I could just stay here and rest a few days, the leg would get better,' he said.

'I'm afraid not,' Sam replied. He knew it was bound to get worse unless it had expert attention. 'Do you think you can manage to ride if we go slow?'

Soak opened eyes red with misery. 'I don't reckon I can, Sheriff,' he said. 'Like as not I'd black out and fall off first thing.'

'We've got another bottle of whiskey to keep you awake.'

'I don't think even whiskey would help me now,' Soak said. It was an amazing admission from him and only served to increase Sam's alarm.

'Then there's only one way,' Sam told him. 'I'll have to tie you in the saddle to make sure nothing like that happens. For we have got to start back.'

The little man grimaced. 'Do what you think best, Sheriff.'

So Sam proceeded with his plan, and not long afterward they began the passage of the difficult trail back to town.

As soon as they got to Grant City, Sam headed directly for Doctor Craig's peaked-roof white house with its green shutters and neat garden. The streets were almost deserted, so he and the stricken Soak attracted little attention. When they arrived in front of the doctor's house, he dropped from the saddle and, after hitching the horses, made his way to the front door.

The young doctor must have seen him, for the door opened before he could knock. Doc Craig studied him with startled eyes and said, 'You look as if you've been through some serious trouble.'

'My friend,' Sam said, breathing heavily. 'He's hurt bad.'

The doctor's eyebrows rose. 'In worse shape than you?'

Sam nodded. 'Got to get him inside,' he said, and waved toward the slumped figure of Soak on his horse.

'Damnation!' Doc Craig said with a

whistle, and hurried out in shirtsleeves and vest to help Sam get the injured man down from his mount.

It was a full half-hour later before Doc Craig faced Sam in his office with a report on the deputy's condition. Doc Craig was a solemn-faced young man who wore a full black beard to give him added dignity. He looked even more serious than usual at the moment.

'I can't guarantee he'll live,' the doctor told Sam. 'And if he does live, I won't promise that I can save that leg.'

'I was afraid of that,' Sam said.

'It's badly infected, and he's in poor shape generally,' Doc Craig went on. 'One way or another, it looks as if he's apt to die within the next twenty-four hours. So I may as well put off amputating until we see what happens.'

'Do what you can for him, Doctor,' Sam begged.

The young man offered him a sharp look. 'That's my job,' he said. 'Right now I think you can do with a few minutes of my attention yourself. Sit down in that chair.'

There was an air of authority in the young doctor's voice that couldn't be ignored. So Sam submitted to the painful ministrations required to clean the scalp wound.

'Good job whoever opened fire on you wasn't a crack shot, Sheriff,' the young doctor said dryly as he finished. 'Otherwise we'd be planting you alongside your brother.'

'I have a lucky streak,' Sam said with a wry smile as he got up.

Doc Craig glanced up from the basin where he was washing his hands. 'I wouldn't strain it if I were you.'

'Thanks, I'll keep that in mind.'

The bearded young medico reached for a towel. 'Whatever induced you to take over as sheriff after what happened to your brother?'

Sam's face clouded. 'It's because of what happened that I did it.'

'You must be a very brave man.' Having finished drying his hands, the doctor threw the towel aside and stood studying Sam with some irony.

'Anything else but,' Sam said. 'But there are some things you just can't run away from.'

'Judging by what happened to you and your deputy last night, running might be the wisest thing you could do.'

'I'm not so sure but that you're right,' Sam was quick to agree. 'But I'm going to stay in Grant City.'

The doctor raised his eyebrows at that. 'I guess we all do what we have to do,' he said. 'But don't count on me for miracles. Better keep out of the range of any hot lead for a while.'

Sam smiled. 'That's good advice. I'll try

and follow it.' He hesitated. 'When can I come back to check on Soak?'

'Later tonight, if you like,' Doc Craig said. 'I finish my office hours at eight. If you come around then, I should know if there is any immediate change in his condition.'

'I'll be around,' Sam promised, and started for the door.

In the jail, Deputy Wade Smith jumped up from his swivel chair and came forward with considerable agitation in his manner.

'I been hoping you'd get back, Sheriff,' the old man with the drooping gray mustache said, 'though I didn't expect you for two or three more days at least.' Then, staring at the open door behind Sam, he asked, 'Where's Soak?'

'At Doc Craig's,' he told him. 'He got a bullet in his leg. That's why I'm back early.' He took off his Stetson so the deputy could see his bandaged head. 'I got a scratch myself.'

'Looks like a mighty deep one,' Deputy Wade Smith said, looking pale. 'I knew you two made a mistake going up to the mine. What happened?'

Sam described what had taken place as briefly as he could. Then he asked the old man, 'What about you? Did you patrol the town last night?'

Deputy Wade Smith looked slightly guilty. 'I went in for a half-hour, but I didn't stay.'

'I see,' Sam said with some disgust. It was what he'd expected to hear.

'Lean Jim Slade was looking for you,' the deputy went on. 'Said you'd told him you'd be by.'

'I did,' Sam remembered. 'I'll be going to the Longhorn now that I'm back.'

'You better,' the old man agreed. 'He appeared right anxious to talk with you.'

'Did you tell him where I was?'

Deputy Wade Smith tugged at his mustache. 'I don't rightly remember. I might have.'

'It would have been better if you just said I was called out of town,' Sam told him. 'You needn't be so ready with information.'

The old man's cheeks went red. 'Sorry, Sheriff.'

Sam regarded him impatiently. 'Anything else?'

'Jack O'Rorke came by looking for you,' the deputy said. 'He wanted me to tell you he'd had complaints about cattle being stolen from a couple of the small ranches.'

'Is that all?'

'Nope,' the old man said with a sigh. 'The Circle 3 was raided again late last night. Jim Halliday was in to see the mayor about it this morning, and the mayor wants to talk to you.'

CHAPTER EIGHT

When Sam entered Mayor Steve Randall's private office about an hour later, the pleasant-faced man looked up from his desk with an expression of surprise and waved him to a chair.

'Sit down, Sheriff,' he said. 'From what Deputy Smith told me, I wasn't expecting to see you back in town today.'

'I ran into some trouble,' Sam said, removing his Stetson so the mayor could see the bandage on his head.

Steve Randall whistled softly and leaned forward, his hands clasped on his desk. 'So you did!' he said. 'When did that happen?'

Sam told him, and also told him about Soak. 'He may not make it,' he said.

Mayor Randall frowned. 'Poor old Soak! Your brother let him go some time ago. But of course you've heard that story.'

'He has a weakness for booze,' Sam said, 'but I wouldn't want to ride with a better lawman.'

'It's most unfortunate that this should have occurred when you were doing so well,' the mayor said. 'You've heard about the latest cattle raid?'

'I reckon that was where Bull Bender and his boys were heading when they left the mine area last night,' Sam told him. 'Somebody must have tipped them off we were coming. They waited for us, and when they thought they had cooked our goose, they came back here to hit the Circle 3 again.'

'Probably so,' the mayor agreed. 'Jim Halliday was in first thing this morning, raising particular cain and asking me to bring a lawman from Abilene.'

Sam raised an eyebrow. 'Do they breed a special brand up there?'

The mayor made an impatient gesture. 'It's just an idea of Halliday's. I told him I intended to give you time to prove yourself, and he stomped out in his usual rage.'

Sam sat back in his chair. 'The big thing Jim Halliday has against me is what I did to his son.'

'I'll go along with that,' the mayor agreed with a frown. 'But from all the reports I've heard, Ben asked for what he got. He's been raised to think Grant City belongs to him. It's time he found out differently.'

'I understand he's done a lot of gambling both here and in Arvilla,' Sam suggested. 'Does his father always pay his debts?'

'There have been some bad arguments between those two,' the mayor admitted. 'But old Jim always pays up for Ben in the end. I hear the boy has lost plenty to Jim Slade at the Longhorn.'

'So have I,' Sam agreed. And giving the

mayor a knowing look, he added, 'I wondered if maybe Ben might have decided to earn some side money for his gambling by tipping off the rustlers when they could safely come in and take some of the Circle 3's stock.'

The mayor showed alarm. 'Don't ever let his father hear you saying that!'

Sam shrugged. 'Jim Halliday was quick enough to accuse Joel of being in on the rustling. And he's kept doing it even since Joel's killing. I don't see why I should worry about his sensitive feelings.'

'I understand your point of view, but don't rile Jim Halliday any more than you have to,' the mayor said, 'specially if you plan to remain in this country any length of time. He's a powerful man!'

'Too powerful to pay attention to the law!'

'Maybe powerful enough to create his own law.'

'I'll keep a sharp eye on Ben,' Sam said.

'Do that,' the mayor agreed. 'But don't noise it about that you think he may be stealing from his own father. Anyway, I don't think he is.'

'What makes you so sure?'

The mayor looked unhappy and stared down at his desk top. 'Ben is a wild, spoiled young man, capable of a lot of things. But being a thief is not among them.'

'You could be right,' Sam said. 'But I'm going to watch a lot of people in this town until I know who is behind all this trouble. Anyway, Barney Wales is eliminated from the list. He drowned himself as neat as you like.'

The mayor sighed. 'Another sad business. Wales was as fine a young man as you'd want to know when he first came here. He had quite an interest in Laura Thorpe, and I thought it might be a match until he got all tangled up in that mining business.'

'I didn't know that,' Sam said, interested.

'Laura would have made him a good wife, but I guess she was as disgusted as the rest of us when Wales developed gold fever,' Mayor Steve Randall said. 'I warned him that the men who had owned the mine first lost all they put into it. But he wouldn't listen to me. Every time he returned to Grant City, he looked more gaunt. You could almost watch his madness grow.' The mayor shrugged. 'Poor fellow! At least his troubles are over.'

'It's too bad I didn't have a chance to talk with him,' Sam said. 'Crazy as he was, he knew what was going on up there. He tried to tell Joel. And Joel's dying words were about some warning Barney Wales gave him.'

'At least you now know Bull Bender is one of the men you're looking for.'

'One of them. There are two others and whoever is behind the whole rotten business.'

The mayor frowned. 'I'm not certain I agree with you there is anyone masterminding the rustling and killings. It doesn't take a great intellect to steal cattle or handle a six-gun. I'd say Bull Bender is qualified to do both, and it has been public knowledge for a long while that he's been nothing less than an outlaw.'

'You may be right,' Sam said, 'but I doubt it. I hear Jack O'Rorke was looking for me as well.' He got up to go.

The mayor rose, saying, 'Yes. About some cattle stolen from several of the farm owners. Very small losses compared to what's been happening at the Circle 3.'

'But no doubt big enough when you consider their small herds,' Sam reminded him.

The mayor looked embarrassed. 'Yes, of course. You're quite right.' He followed him to the door. 'You know I'm strongly behind you in all that you do. But I must beg you to be discreet. I am subject to certain pressure.'

Sam turned at the door with a sarcastic smile. 'Halliday and Cameron, I suppose.'

'Since you know your opposition so well, you should understand why you must proceed carefully.'

'I don't think I can settle this by being careful.'

The mayor sighed. 'I mentioned that I told Halliday I intended to give you all the time necessary to prove yourself.' He hesitated. 'But there is also another side to it. If you make any really grave error, I'll be forced to ask for that star back at once.'

'You mean like accusing Ben Halliday of being in with the rustlers?'

'That could eliminate you from the picture.'

'I'll keep that in mind,' Sam said in a tone that indicated that he wouldn't let the warning change his plans in any way. And he left the mayor's office without any further comment.

Since it was dinner time, he rode on to the house and found Aunt Maggie up and about again, with a meal ready on the stove for him. The little old woman beamed at him fondly.

'Somehow I knew you'd be here for dinner tonight,' she said. 'I've got your favorite. Beef stew!'

It was good to sit in the big kitchen again and listen to Aunt Maggie's gossip as he enjoyed the excellent food. The old woman seemed to have partially recovered from the shock of Joel's death, although the sadness it had brought her was clearly pictured in her wrinkled face.

With dinner out of the way, he decided to make his rounds of the town. His first stop would be the Longhorn Saloon, since Jim Slade had been inquiring about him. He'd asked the gambler to try to get him some information without being particularly hopeful that he would succeed. Now it looked as if Slade had turned up with something.

Dusk was beginning to fall when he tied the roan to the hitching post outside the Longhorn. The number of horses hitched there indicated the saloon must be doing a healthy business. The old-timer he'd seen Soak talking to on several occasions was standing before the swinging doors, and when Sam stepped up on the wooden sidewalk, the white-bearded man buttonholed him.

'Hear Soak is in a bad way,' he said dolefully, peering up at Sam.

'I think he still has a good chance,' Sam said, wanting to sound hopeful even if he didn't feel that way.

'I hope you get the varmints that plugged him!' the old-timer said.

Sam patted the old man's shoulder. 'I've got their names on my list.'

'Your brother was a first rate sheriff, and I'll bet you will be, too,' the old man called after him as he pushed his way through the swinging doors and found himself in the noisy, smoke-polluted interior of the Longhorn.

The piano player was on the stage, beating out gay tunes on the ivories. A majority of the tables were already filled, and there was a good line at the bar. A glance toward the main gambling table over which Lean Jim Slade invariably presided showed him it was empty. The big game usually didn't begin until later in the evening, Sam remembered.

Deciding to fill in some time, he took a place at the bar under his favorite painting. The bartender came down to serve him at once.

'What'll it be tonight, Sheriff?' the shirt-sleeved man asked respectfully.

'Whiskey straight!' Sam told him.

'You bet, Sheriff.' The bartender was all politeness. He filled a glass and set it out for Sam, with the bottle beside it for refills as required.

'The boss around?' Sam inquired.

'Expect him any minute,' the bartender said.

Sam downed the whiskey and poured himself a second one. Then he glanced around to study the smoke-filled main room. He noticed the cowpoke named Buck from the Circle 3 was seated at a rear table. He had three other men with him, and they were all keeping their eyes fixed on the bar. Sam had an idea he was the main object of their attention and wondered if he was going to have more trouble with Ben Halliday and his cronies.

His consideration of this was interrupted when Lean Jim Slade came briskly through the swinging doors. He was wearing a smartly tailored gray pearl suit and a top hat to match. These items, along with his wing collar, rich black cravat and diamond stickpin, gave him the air of careless elegance which was clearly his goal. When he saw Sam at the bar, a smile crossed his thin face and he came straight across to him.

'Delightful surprise, Sheriff,' he said. 'They told me I wouldn't be seeing you for days.'

'I came back early,' Sam told him. 'I understand you've been looking for me.'

'That is quite correct,' the gambler said suavely. With a look of distaste at their surroundings, he added, 'I think we can talk to better advantage in my private office.'

'Okay,' Sam said, and reached in his pocket for coins to pay for his drinks.

'Not in my place,' Lean Jim Slade told him, and at the same time pressed a black cane with a silver head across Sam's hand to restrain him from paying.

Sam's eyebrows raised. 'I like to pay my way,' he said.

'It's a policy of the house not to charge the law,' Slade said with a smile of his narrow face. 'Sorry we can't make exceptions for you, Sheriff.'

So it was settled. Sam put the cash back in his pocket and followed the thin man down to the office at the rear of the long room, knowing that countless eyes were on them.

Lean Jim Slade's office was larger than Sam had expected and richly furnished. The walls were done in crimson paper with a small pattern of black; the carpet on the floor was a matching crimson. The desk and other items of furniture were of mahogany, and an elaborate crystal chandelier hung from the ceiling directly in the center of the room, with four lamps set in it to give the entire room a soft but brilliant illumination. The gambler glanced with satisfaction at Sam as he closed the door to give them privacy.

'You like it?' he wanted to know.

'It's mighty classy,' Sam said, impressed.

'Spent more on it than I should,' Lean Jim Slade said, giving the setting an appreciative look that suggested he wasn't sorry he'd been extravagant.

'You like to have things nice,' Sam said.

Slade nodded. 'I'll admit that.' He stood behind his desk and, removing first his top hat and then his gloves, placed them to one side of the desk. He smiled at Sam again as he held up the silver-headed cane for inspection. 'I suppose you consider it a little ridiculous for me to carry a walking stick.'

'It's your own business.'

'It is, indeed.' The fox-like face of the gambler showed a look of secret amusement. 'But a walking stick can be extremely handy. You see!' He accompanied his words by pulling off the silver head with a swift motion: now he was holding a sword-like blade about a foot long in his hand.

Sam stared at the blade. 'Neat,' he said.

'I think so,' Lean Jim Slade agreed, and with the same deftness shoved the blade back in the concealment of the walking stick. 'You'd be surprised how many tight places it has gotten me out of.'

'Probably,' Sam was ready to agree. 'But I don't suppose you brought me here just to show me that.'

'No, of course not,' the gambler said briskly, putting the walking stick to one side. 'Please make yourself comfortable, Sheriff. You look rather gaunt tonight. No doubt the strain of your injury.'

Sam sank into one of the upholstered chairs facing the saloon owner's desk. 'You know all about it?'

'Yes.' The gambler smiled. 'From a very direct source, I might add.'

'Bull Bender?'

'I don't think there is any need to beat about the bush. To be frank, yes. The Bull did speak to me concerning the incident.'

Sam frowned. 'You're not fussy about your choice of friends.'

'How can I be?' Slade wanted to know. He settled back in his swivel chair. 'I'm in a rough business and bound to meet unpleasant people. I hasten to add that I am not associated in any enterprise with the gentleman in question. But he has an odd habit of confiding in me.'

'He was in town to strike at the Circle 3 again,' Sam said.

Slade made a delicate gesture with a slim

hand. 'Precisely,' he said.

'You know plenty about his doings for somebody who has no interest in them,' Sam pointed out.

'He's a crass fellow,' Slade deplored. 'I tolerate boors at the gambling table, since they make easy prey. But I avoid having any other business dealings with them.'

'Do you know the names of the two men riding with Bender?'

'Of course.' The narrow face showed amusement. 'I am very well informed. 'One of them is a Mexican called Carlos Ramez, and the other is a tough from Dodge City who answers to the name of Burt Samson. I happen to know it isn't his real name, but that is unimportant. They were the men who shot down your brother and tried to finish off you and Soak Dooley.'

'Why?'

'Because both you and your brother offered a threat to them.' He shook his head sadly. 'Joel's killing should have warned you. You've made a bad mistake grabbing onto that star. The town's good citizens aren't convinced you are on the level, and the bad ones are just as certain you are. You can't win!'

Sam stared at the smiling gambler. 'Why are you being so helpful with information?'

'I thought you'd get around to that.'

'I'm mighty interested,' Sam said grimly. 'I

don't see what you've got to gain, unless you're in with Bull Bender and the others and this is some kind of trick play.'

'You're quite wrong in assuming that, I assure you.'

'What then?'

'I have purposely refrained from revealing my position in all this until I provide you with the complete picture,' Slade said in his suave way. 'But I can tell you this much. I happen to be an ambitious man, and I am sure that in assisting you in this matter I'll be indirectly helping myself.'

Sam's voice took on a sharp edge. 'I think I warned you once before, Slade. I don't intend to be a party to any of your crooked deals.'

The gambler did not appear upset. 'But, of course, Sheriff. I have far too high a regard for your principles even to suggest such a thing.'

'Then I don't see what you have to gain.'

Lean Jim Slade's expression was mocking. 'That is because you lack my perception. You do not see the picture as a whole. When it is all settled, you will know that I have been completely truthful with you.'

'In that case, where are Bender and his henchmen now?'

'Following a secret trail to Abilene with a choice selection of stock from the Circle 3 and a couple of the smaller ranches.'

'Which they'll sell there as Cactus 8 brand

beef!'

'Exactly.'

Sam stood up. 'All right! Give me a plan of the route they're taking and full information on how many men are in the outfit and where I can best halt them.'

The gambler looked mildly startled. 'Now you are giving me orders!'

'You've admitted you know all about the rustling. If you're on the level with me, you won't hold back the answers to my questions.'

'I don't intend to refuse,' Slade admitted. 'Otherwise I wouldn't have exposed my hand to this extent. But I reserve the right to inform you in my own good time.'

Sam came close to the desk, anger in his blue eyes. 'I want to know now!'

There was a moment's silence, and then the gambler gave him a pitying smile. 'You're much too direct, you know,' he said with mock sympathy. 'That sort of approach gets you nowhere. I have been generous enough to provide you with an enormous fund of information, and you show your gratitude by bullying me.'

'I'm sorry,' Sam said. 'I haven't your gift for fancy words.'

'Nor my ability to think clearly. In your bovine haste for information, you've forgotten the most important item of all.'

'And that is?'

'Who is really behind the organized rustling?'

Sam eyed him closely. 'Not Bender?'

Lean Jim Slade was disdainful. 'Even you know that.'

'Who then?'

'That I am not prepared to reveal at the moment.'

Sam glared at the gambler in angry defiance. 'I think you're playing a game with me, Slade. If so, let me warn you that you've gone too far.'

The gambler rose to his feet and regarded Sam coldly. 'And let me warn you to keep a civil tongue if you expect to have my continued cooperation. I'm beginning to regret my trust in you.'

Seeing that nothing was to be gained by threatening the thin man, Sam decided to curb his impatience and let Slade do things his way. He shrugged. 'All right. I'll go along with you. When do you plan to let me in on your secrets?'

Slade beamed happily. 'Now you begin to sound like a civilized human being. I have reason to believe I can offer you complete information by eleven o'clock tonight. You meet me here. Come in by the back door that leads directly to the office, if you'd prefer not to be seen in the saloon again.'

'I like the idea,' Sam said. 'I'll be here at eleven.'

'Then we have nothing further to discuss now,' Slade said.

Sam hesitated at the desk. 'I think I see why you're making me wait until eleven.'

'Really?' The gambler was enjoying himself again.

'You've offered a deal to the other party,' Sam suggested. 'If they come through with the pay-off you want, you'll refuse to expose them to me. You've already informed them that you've talked to me, and warned that you'll tell me the rest of the story if they won't pay your price.'

'You've summed it up very neatly, Sheriff,' Lean Jim Slade said. 'No matter what happens, I'm holding a trump hand.'

'If you get your pay-off, you'll have nothing to offer me at eleven!'

'You underestimate me, my dear fellow,' the gambler said. 'You shall have the hospitality of the house—as much of my best whiskey as you can drink.'

Sam shook his head in disgust. 'I might have known you were using me as a means to get your price. But don't forget you've pinned the rustling on Bull Bender and his cronies.'

Slade laughed. 'You're welcome to that, Sheriff. They are only the pawns in the game. They can be easily sacrificed and just as easily replaced.' He went over and opened the door to show him out. 'Until eleven then, Sheriff. And who knows? You may be in luck.'

CHAPTER NINE

Sam made his exit from the office of the Longhorn's owner, feeling frustrated and angered. Lean Jim Slade had not bothered to conceal the fact he was using him as a decoy. Yet because the situation was so complicated, he had no alternative but to play along with the gambler. He had learned enough to take action against Bull Bender and his henchmen, although he had a shrewd idea Slade would go back on his testimony if put in a spot where he had to accuse Bender directly.

So it could be he had gained nothing, while Slade was in a position to win a big pay-off if his wily moves were successful. He stood for a moment in the busy saloon and let his eyes wander to the table where Buck and the Circle 3 crowd had been gathered. They had left while he was talking to Slade, and the table was empty now. He realized it was after eight o'clock and time to stop by the doctor's again to find out how Soak Dooley was doing.

With this in mind, he made his way to the door of the saloon. The street was busier now, and lights had appeared in all of the shop windows. He strode down the board sidewalk until he came to the doctor's house. There was a lamp on a table near the front window, but no sign of anyone inside. He knocked on the door and tried the handle. It wasn't locked, so he stepped into the office. It was empty, but a moment later a rear door opened and a pretty, dark-haired woman in her thirties emerged.

'The doctor is out on a call,' she informed him. 'He doesn't have office hours after eight.'

Sam removed his Stetson. 'It isn't about myself I came,' he said. 'He told me I could come back to find out about my friend, Soak Dooley.'

The woman at once became more friendly. 'I didn't notice your badge, Sheriff. My husband mentioned you might be in. I'm afraid there's been no real change in Mr. Dooley's condition.'

'But he's no worse?'

'He's no worse, and I suppose, in a sense, that is good news.'

'Thanks, ma'am,' he said. 'I'm sorry to have troubled you. Soak is lucky the doctor took him in and you're here to nurse him.'

'We couldn't turn him away,' the doctor's wife said. 'He's a very sick man. The doctor may have to remove his leg if he doesn't show improvement by tomorrow.'

Sam frowned. 'When will you know?'

'By early afternoon,' the woman said. 'Why don't you call again then?'

'I will,' he promised. 'And if Soak asks, tell him I've been here.'

She nodded. 'I will. He hasn't been able to talk at all. The doctor has kept him under heavy sedation.'

Sam went back into the street with a sick heart. It had been another unhappy interview.

He was so lost in his somber reverie he did not hear the carriage coming up by him and halting. And he turned only when he heard his name uttered in a female voice.

'Sam, how wonderful! I've been thinking about you, and there you are!' It was Laura Thorpe holding the reins in the carriage. She bent forward to him with a smile on her lovely face.

Sam doffed his Stetson. 'Guess I was doing some wool-gathering,' he said.

Laura gave him an arch look. 'As sheriff of Grant City, that's a luxury you can't afford unless you want to wind up with a slug in your back. I heard about Soak,' she said, with a nod toward the doctor's place. 'Is he any better?'

'No change.'

'That's too bad,' she said. And then, in a different mood, 'I've so many things to say to you, Sam. Why don't we go for a short drive before I go to the saloon?'

Putting on his Stetson, he swung up onto the carriage seat beside her. 'I can't take long,' he said.

'Nor can I,' she told him. 'But we can steal

a few minutes, surely.' She offered him a warm smile. 'You take the reins.'

He did, and let the big chestnut mare go along at its own trotting gait. Within a few minutes they had left the busiest section of the main business street and were rapidly reaching the outskirts of the frontier city.

Laura glanced skyward at the quarter-moon. 'At least there is some moonlight,' she said.

'I haven't had time to notice.'

'It seems to me you're missing a lot of things you may regret,' she told him. 'I understand you had a close call yourself last night.'

'I wasn't hit nearly as bad as Soak,' he said.

She gave a deep sigh. 'I think that was mere luck. And it may not last. Why don't you give up this crazy business, Sam? Let Grant City pick on someone else for sheriff.'

He gave her a glance, smiling wryly. 'Is that what you brought me out here in the moonlight to tell me?'

'That and a few other things. Let's stop the carriage here and walk for a while. I can't think while we're driving.'

He noted they were passing through an area of broad open fields. Pulling the mare up short, he jumped down from the carriage and hobbled her so she would not stray. Then he helped Laura Thorpe from the carriage, easing her gently to the ground. She faced him with shining eyes.

'Life could hold so much for us, Sam,' she said softly, 'if only you weren't so stubborn.'

He shook his head. 'You're a lovely girl, and no man in his right mind could fail to be attracted to you. But that doesn't mean you and I are in love.'

'Love!' Laura said angrily. 'What special value is there in that word? People use it as an excuse for every kind of madness. I married without love, and it turned out very well. Pleasure, money, passion are all words that make a lot more sense to me! We could have a wonderful life together, Sam, if we could get away from this town where I'm Bruce Thorpe's widow and you're Joel Wallace's brother and people won't let either of us be anything else!'

'It's an attractive idea, Laura,' he said with a sigh. 'But I know we'd both soon tire of each other. And wasn't it Joel you really wanted, anyway?'

'Joel is dead,' she said in a suddenly flat tone. 'I've learned not to dream of the dead.' She looked at him earnestly. 'Joel was a fool! I warned him, but he wouldn't listen to me! You don't have to make the same mistake. Turn in your badge and head for Abilene. I'll join you there in a few weeks, and we can be married and go East!'

He shook his head. 'Let's not rush into anything.'

Her eyes shone with anger. 'It's Virginia Cameron, isn't it? That's why you're putting on this brave hero show! That's who you want to marry—the banker's meek little daughter!'

'You're being unfair!' he protested. 'Let's leave Virginia out of this.'

'That's the way Joel talked,' Laura raged. 'And you see where it got him!'

'Joel was killed because of his feud with the rustlers; not because he loved Virginia and married her,' Sam said. 'And it may be that I'll be turning in my badge whether I want to or not.'

Laura's anger gave way to curiosity. 'Why do you say that?'

'There are a lot of people against me,' he explained. 'Jim Halliday and his son. Charles Cameron, for another. The mayor told me he's under pressure to let me go, so it could happen any time.'

'You see?' Laura argued. 'Doesn't that convince you you're being a fool to stay on here?'

'I may be a fool,' he said. 'But I'm a fool with a purpose. I want to settle the score for Joel, and now there's a small account for Soak Dooley as well. First I'm going to round up Bull Bender and his crowd, and after that whoever is behind him.'

'You'll never live to do it!' she said bitterly.

'I may have a better chance than you

think,' he told her. 'Jim Slade has given me some information. He knows the story behind the rustling. And before the night is over, he may give me the name of the person I want, the name of the one who planned all this foolishness. I'm to see him at eleven o'clock.'

Her lovely face showed doubt. 'You can't trust Slade!'

'I can in this,' he said carefully. 'According to Slade, he has something to gain by working with me.'

Laura bowed her head and turned away from him. 'He'll lead you on and trick you in the end.'

'I know that can happen,' he agreed. 'But I've so little to go on. I have to follow every lead.'

She began to stroll slowly through the field, and he followed a pace behind her. Both of them were silent, occupied with their own brooding thoughts. At last the lovely young widow turned to him.

'Sam, will you promise me at least one thing? If Slade double-crosses you, will you agree to give it all up?'

'I'd still have to settle with Bender.'

'All right,' she said wearily. 'You'll settle with Bender, providing you can find him. Then will you go to Abilene and wait for me?'

He smiled at her. 'It's an inviting offer. I'll sure give it plenty of thought.'

'Oh, Sam!' she said softly, and came into

his arms again.

They said little on the way back. Laura appeared to be content with what she considered his promise, although he had actually been careful not to give her any real answer.

It was close to ten when they drove up before the Grant City Saloon. Laura Thorpe seemed to be suddenly nervous. 'We talked too long,' she said. 'I'm late getting here.'

'I'll take the carriage around to the livery stable for you,' Sam said, helping her to the board sidewalk. He was conscious of the stares of the loiterers around the entrance to the saloon.

Laura smiled up at him. 'Thanks, Sam. That will help. Come by and see me when you can.'

'Don't worry about that,' he told her. He watched as she hurried on into the noisy saloon, then climbed back into the carriage again and drove in the direction of the livery stable. It was located behind the hotel, and a long dark alley led to it.

When he arrived there, only one stable boy was on duty; he quickly took over and promised to take care of the horse and carriage. Sam headed back down the shadowy alley, planning to return to the main street and pick up the roan which he'd left hitched in front of the Longhorn Saloon nearly two hours before.

Suddenly he clearly heard the sound of a heavy footstep on the gravel just in front of him. Alerted to possible danger, he peered into the darkness ahead and at the same time reached for his Colt. There was the sound of other footsteps now, and an icy fear shot through him as he was warned by the sixth sense he'd developed that this could mean serious trouble for him. He raised the Colt slowly as a huge figure was dimly outlined in the shadows before him.

Then the phantom figure spoke. 'Hello, Sheriff.' The words came in a lazy venomous drawl, and he recognized the voice as Ben Halliday's.

He stopped dead, and Ben Halliday also stood motionless a few feet from him. With the Colt still drawn, Sam asked, 'What do you want, Ben?'

'That's kind of a crazy question, Sheriff,' young Halliday went on in his insolent patronizing way.

Sam knew the son of the owner of the Circle 3 was out for revenge. And he was acutely aware of his isolated position in the dark alley. He was certain that Ben had his cronies with him and knew he'd walked into an ambush. His only advantage was that he had his gun, and right now it was covering Ben Halliday. Not that he'd dare to fire at the young bully unless he had good reason. If he did, he knew Jim Halliday would see there was a rope stretching his neck in no time.

'If you have anything to say to me, we can discuss it on the street or in the saloon,' he told Ben.

The young man gave a nasty laugh. 'We'll discuss it right here, Sheriff.' And then in a sharp command: 'All right, Buck!'

Before Sam could use his Colt, he was gripped fiercely from behind. He pressed the trigger, but the bullet went far wide of its target. As he struggled, staggering backward in the grip of his assailant, he was struck a stunning blow on the head by a gun butt in another's hands, and his grip on his own weapon loosened as still a different hand tore it from his grasp. Now he was unarmed!

Still he fought savagely to get free as his head cleared. The blow had caught him near the place of the bullet wound, and he was suffering agonizing pain that slowed down his efforts to save himself. At last his strength was exhausted, and he found himself held there by many unseen hands, his breath coming in slow gasps as he defiantly faced Ben Halliday.

'All right, Mr. Sheriff,' Ben Halliday said softly. 'Now you'll find out I've still got a good left hand!' He followed his words by directing a great walloping blow into Sam's face. It caught him high on the cheekbone, broke skin and drew blood. Young Halliday roared with delight and sent another punishing left that caught Sam on the mouth and set it to bleeding.

Again he struggled wildly to free himself from the restraining hands and at the same time tried to dodge the rain of blows Ben Halliday was driving at him with insane fury. Luckily, he did manage to avoid some of the worst of the punches. But now one caught him at the outer edge of his left eye and sent blood spurting. He knew Ben Halliday had no intention of letting up until his face was a bruised and bleeding pulp. His only salvation was his continued resistance, and he was acutely aware that his strength was ebbing rapidly. In a moment or two he would slide into unconsciousness, and the vengeful fist of the young bully would finish its grim task with ease.

'What's going on down there?' a voice cried from close by.

Ben Halliday whispered hoarsely. 'All right, boys! Let's go!'

As quickly as he'd been seized, Ben was let go. The hands that had held him so tightly let him drop to the ground, and he dully heard the scurry of their retreat. He fell face forward on the hard gravel and then raised himself a little on his hands.

Other footsteps came running up to him, and an urgent voice asked, 'You hurt bad?'

He took a deep breath and shook his head. 'No, thanks to you.'

'It's you, Sheriff.' Sam recognized the voice as belonging to Jack O'Rorke, the farmers' spokesman.

'You arrived just before the real slaughter,' Sam said weakly as the other man helped him to his feet. 'I was about to pass out, and then they would have done a real job on me.'

'Bunch of cowards!' O'Rorke said with rage in his voice. 'Any idea who they were?'

'Ben Halliday was their leader,' he said, running a hand over his temple.

'Him again!' the other man said. 'He'll never learn his lesson!'

He closed his eyes a moment as he tried to collect his thoughts. 'I'm pretty much of a mess,' he said. 'And I've got a Colt on the ground here somewhere.'

'I'll find it for you,' Jack O'Rorke promised, and after a moment struck a light. By its brief glow they located the Colt a few feet from Sam. He grimly returned it to its holster.

'I should have used it on him first thing,' Sam said. 'But then his father would have dubbed me a killing sheriff.'

'Still, he shouldn't get away with this!'

'He's bound to deny any part of it,' Sam told the other man bitterly. 'And I have no witnesses except you.'

'And I couldn't make anyone out in the darkness,' Jack O'Rorke said with frustration.

'I'd better get myself somewhere and fix my face,' Sam said. 'I've got an important appointment at eleven.'

'There's only one place to go,' O'Rorke told him. 'You need a doctor.'

Doc Craig went about repairing the damages to Sam's face systematically. Jack O'Rorke stood by with a stern expression. At last the young doctor finished treating the cut that had left the sheriff's eye puffed up and nearly closed.

'You begin to make me wonder how much punishment one human can take,' Doc Craig said.

'I don't aim to try finding out any more,' Sam assured him.

'Then you better avoid dark alleys,' was Jack O'Rorke's comment.

'You'll have a nasty eye for a few days,' the doctor warned, 'although a good deal of the swelling ought to vanish by tomorrow.'

'Thanks,' Sam said, picking up his Stetson. 'Soak will be sore when he hears about missing out on this scrap.'

'You can tell him if he rallies tomorrow,' the doctor observed with a faint smile.

When they left the doctor's office, Jack O'Rorke continued to remain with him. The little man appeared much concerned about what had happened. As they stood together outside the Longhorn Saloon, O'Rorke told Sam, 'Attacking a law officer is a serious offense. You ought to be able to think of some way of proving Ben Halliday was the ringleader.'

'It's not going to be easy,' Sam told him.

'I say to charge him anyway,' the farmers' man said indignantly. 'Even if you can't make it stick, they'll know you are onto their game.'

'That might help,' he admitted.

O'Rorke gave him an anxious glance. 'You sound like a man ready to throw in the sponge, Sheriff. I hope that isn't what you have in mind. The farmers and the small ranchers around these parts need you.'

'I'll try to remember that,' he said. 'The Hallidays sure don't want me to stay.'

'Jim Halliday has run this part of Kansas far too long,' O'Rorke complained. 'The days of the big ranchers are numbered. There's a new breed of settler here, and they mean to stay. The small owners I represent will give you all the backing they can. And I think maybe it will be enough.'

'I may need a posse to help round up the rustling gang,' Sam said. 'Do you think you could provide me with a dozen good riders?'

'Just say the word and I'll have them for you,' O'Rorke promised.

'Don't be surprised if I call on you soon,' Sam said.

He left the other man with a feeling of satisfaction. At least he had one good friend in Grant City. And he had the idea Jack O'Rorke stood for a lot more authority than most people in the frontier town realized.

Removing his watch from his vest he saw that it was ten minutes to eleven. He was due to talk to Lean Jim Slade almost any time now. And if his luck held, he might get the information he'd wanted from the beginning: word on who was the brains behind Bull Bender and his crowd of outlaws.

Slade had suggested he use the rear door, but he suddenly realized this meant going the length of the long saloon building by another dark alley. And he had lost his enthusiasm for dark places. He decided he would rather expose his battered face to the patrons of the saloon rather than risk another ambush in the shadows of the alley.

He made his way into the noisy place, ignoring the stares and wise grins of those who noticed his face. The piano music seemed louder and less appealing than usual, and the nightly drunken festival in the Longhorn was at its peak. These were hard, rough men who played in the same rugged manner in which they worked. Sam went down to the door of Lean Jim Slade's private office and tried the handle. The door was locked. He rapped on it lightly and waited. But there was no answer.

Yet the big gambling table was empty, so Slade was not conducting his usual game. He must be somewhere around, or maybe he had gone to talk a deal over with the mystery man. Sam decided to return to the bar and have a whiskey.

The bartender recognized him, and for an instant his bland face showed surprise at the damage inflicted on him by Ben Halliday's savage fists. Then he recovered himself and quickly provided him with a glass and a full bottle of whiskey.

'Help yourself, Sheriff,' he said.

Sam drained his glass and felt better. 'Where's the boss?' he asked.

The bartender jerked his head toward the rear of the building. 'In his office.'

'I tried it,' he said. 'It's locked, and he didn't answer.'

The bartender shrugged. 'Maybe he went out the back door.'

'Maybe,' Sam said. He poured himself another drink and downed it. Now he began to regret that he hadn't braved the darkness and followed Slade's instructions by going around to the rear door. He was about to leave the saloon and do this when he saw the door of the private office slowly open. Lean Jim Slade stood in the doorway, staring at the crowd as if he might be looking for someone.

Sam took it as his cue. He hurriedly stepped away from the bar and headed toward the gambler. When he reached him, he said, 'I've been waiting to see you.'

Slade gave him a slight nod, his face strangely pale. He stood there without inviting Sam into the office.

'What's the word?' Sam asked.

Lean Jim Slade's lips moved as if to make a reply, but he said nothing. Instead, he took a step forward and all at once lurched into Sam's arms. As Sam reached to support the gambler, he caught a glimpse of his back. The pearl grey coat showed a wide dark stain, and in its center was a partly imbedded silver-hilted sword: the walking stick weapon Slade had so proudly shown him earlier in the evening.

CHAPTER TEN

Sam stood by the window of the jail and stared out at the rolling fields under the blazing morning sun. It was another day, and Lean Jim Slade was dead. And with him had died most of his hopes of pinning down the rustling gang and its leader. It was the second brutal murder in Grant City within a few days, and there wasn't a question but that Cameron, Halliday and the other dissenters would make the most of it. They wouldn't be slow to inform the mayor how inadequate Sam was for the job he'd taken on after Joel's killing.

From the swivel chair, Deputy Wade Smith gave a great sigh. 'I just can't figure it, Sheriff. Why would anyone want to kill Jim Slade?'

Sam didn't bother to look around at the old man. Still staring out the window with a frown, he said, 'Slade must have had plenty more enemies than the average man. A lot of money was lost at his table.'

'More to it than that,' the deputy said in his rumbling voice. 'Slade has been operating the Longhorn for a good many years. Until last night, he was always able to take care of himself.'

Sam was tempted to say that maybe the gambler knew too much, had found out more than was good for him. But he wanted to keep all the scant information he possessed to himself. He turned to the forlorn figure of Deputy Wade Smith. With a wry expression he said, 'I guess we both ought to resign.'

Smith tugged nervously at his straggly gray mustache. 'My missus has been nagging me to do that for more than a year now.'

Sam studied the old man and in a gentler tone said, 'You might be wise to do it right away. There's every chance there'll soon be bad trouble in Grant City.'

The old deputy shook his head. 'I'm frightened, Sheriff; plumb out of my mind with fear, because I know my shootin' hand ain't steady, my eyes play tricks on me, and I can't use my fists worth a plugged lead dollar. My body is worn out, and I'm no use here any more.' He gave Sam an ashamed glance. 'You'd have done better if I'd given you any backing at all. And maybe if I'd been around as I ought to have been, those outlaws wouldn't have gotten Joel. With Soak Dooley on his back, you're all alone in this, Sheriff.'

Sam was touched by the old man's confession. Going over to him, he laid a hand on his shoulder. 'You've done well enough,' he said. 'I'm glad to have you here.'

Deputy Wade Smith brightened a little. 'You really mean that?'

'Sure I do,' he said. 'I'm going into town now to see how Soak is doing. The doctor is going to decide today whether to cut off his leg or not.'

The old man became gloomy again. 'I sure hope they don't have to do it.'

'So do I,' Sam said. But he knew the odds were that Soak would have to undergo the amputation.

When he arrived at the doctor's office, the black-bearded young man was at his desk. He glanced up at Sam with a gleam of amusement in his eyes.

'You don't actually look handsome today, Sheriff,' he observed with dry humor. 'But you're not such a scary specimen as you were last night, either.'

Sam touched the plaster patch by his eye.

'Thanks to your good services,' he said. 'What I'm really worried about is my friend.'

The doctor got up. 'Seems to me you and your friends are made of solid rawhide. The amount of punishment you can absorb astonishes me. Dooley is a lot better than yesterday. The chances are he'll live and we can save his leg.'

It was doubly good news because Sam had been expecting to hear the worst. A smile came to his thin, tense young face. 'That's wonderful,' he said. 'Can I see him yet?'

Doc Craig nodded. 'Only for a couple of minutes. He still has a long fight ahead.'

'I won't stay, Doc,' Sam promised. 'But I would like to wish the old buzzard good luck.'

The young doctor led him into the back bedroom where a wan Soak Dooley lay. The little man's purple face showed a smile as soon as he spotted Sam. 'You danged near killed me,' he said in a low voice, 'but I aim to fool you yet.'

Sam smiled down at him with genuine affection. 'Sure you will. We'll be riding out together again before you know it.'

'Sure,' the little man said vaguely. And then he added, 'Take care, Sam. Take care!'

Sam left the doctor's filled with relief at the knowledge that Soak Dooley had a good chance to recover. He was also touched by the little man's concern for him. He decided to walk up to the mayor's office and find out what the official reaction might be to Lean Jim Slade's killing. But he had gone only a few steps when he saw a familiar figure coming down the sidewalk toward him. It was Jim Halliday, the owner of the Circle 3, and he had a mean expression.

When Sam came up to him, he decided to tackle him about Ben then and there. Halting, he said, 'Good morning, Mr. Halliday. I've got something to say to you.'

The big man drew himself up with a regal air and scowled at him. 'Nothing I want to hear. You may as well know I don't look on you as sheriff, and I aim to see that you're replaced at the next council meeting.'

'Whatever your views about me,' Sam said quietly, 'I'd say you should be more concerned about your son.'

'I should think you'd keep Ben out of this,' big Jim Halliday said angrily, 'after what you did to him.'

'If you take a close look at my face, you'll see what Ben and some of his cronies did to me last night,' Sam said. 'He organized a gang attack on me in a dark alley, and while his men held me he pounded my face.'

The ranch owner's eyes bulged with fury. 'You dare accuse Ben of such a cowardly act?'

'I not only accuse him; I may charge him with it,' he bluffed. 'It so happens I have a witness who came to my rescue. As you know, sir, that kind of attack is a pretty serious business.'

Jim Halliday swallowed hard. 'Ben didn't leave the ranch all last night,' he said at last.

'I could probably prove you're wrong about that as well,' Sam said calmly.

'You'd do better to bring a halt to the cattle raiding or find your brother's killer and Jim Slade's than to threaten my son,' the big man said, but Sam could see he was shaken.

'I don't think you're a bad man, Halliday,' Sam said earnestly. 'And I doubt you intended to raise a son as spoiled as Ben. I can only warn you that if he goes on without regard for the law, he's bound to involve both you and himself in a lot of trouble.'

The big man studied him with a confused expression on his arrogant face. He seemed ready to say something, then clamped his mouth shut grimly as if he'd suddenly changed his mind. Without any word of reply, he strode on past Sam.

When Sam reached the mayor's office, he found Steve Randall standing by the window that looked out on the street with a hint of grim amusement on his face. He removed a cigar from his mouth to say, 'I saw you and Jim Halliday tangle a few minutes ago.'

'That's right,' Sam said. And he proceeded to tell him what the discussion had been about, ending with, 'Let's hope from now on he'll keep a stricter rein on young Ben.'

'From what you've told me, I have no question that he will.' The mayor frowned as he studied Sam's battered features. 'I don't know but what you ought to charge him and put him in jail anyway.'

'No use. I couldn't make it stick.'

'Seems like the law isn't able to pin anything on anybody in this town,' the mayor said, puffing angrily on his cigar. 'Now we've got a new murder to solve.'

'Slade must have been killed by someone he knew,' Sam ventured slowly. 'It had to be somebody he trusted and didn't suspect of violence; also somebody who knew the secret of that walking stick. If Slade had had the least suspicion, he wouldn't have let him within a foot of it.'

The mayor studied the spiral of drifting blue smoke from his cigar with narrowed eyes. 'Somebody he knew and trusted,' he said. 'Somebody who stabbed him in the back.'

'It cuts down the suspects considerably,' Sam pointed out.

'So it does,' the mayor agreed, '*if* your theory is right.'

'It couldn't have been the work of a casual intruder,' Sam argued. 'For one thing, there is nothing to suggest robbery. No money was taken, though there was a considerable amount in one of the desk drawers.'

'Somebody might have killed him for

revenge.'

'Revenge for what?'

The mayor shrugged. 'You tell me. Slade must have had lots of enemies.'

Sam gave him a wry smile. 'Judging from what I've heard around town this morning, I'd say he didn't. Most people liked him. His card game was no different from those operated in saloons all over the West, and he ran his place with very little trouble.'

The mayor nodded in mild surprise. 'I never looked at it exactly that way,' he agreed. 'But you're right. Both saloons in town have been well operated. We'll be lucky if some crook doesn't take over and bring us a lot of extra grief.'

'I have news for you,' Sam told him. 'From what I understand, Laura Thorpe is ready to make an offer for the place. She had Cameron go over there today and talk to his manager. Seems that Slade has an heir, a sister somewhere in California.'

'I hope Laura gets it,' the mayor said, looking happier. 'That would solve that problem.'

They talked a little while longer, and then Sam left him. He rode over to the jail and checked with Deputy Wade Smith. There were no messages, and he decided he would make a visit to Arvilla. He had been thinking a good deal about Virginia, and this might be his last free chance to go to the adjoining town for a while. He checked with the old deputy, who knew her aunt's name. And with that information, he mounted the roan and headed out of town.

The only thing Sam met on the road was the afternoon stage. The driver waved in passing, and he returned the greeting. The day was warmer than usual, and he didn't urge the roan at too fast a pace.

Arvilla was a sleepy little town, smaller than Grant City. It was late afternoon when Sam arrived there, and he went straight to the far end of the settlement where the deputy had told him Virginia's aunt lived. It was a section of better homes, and he had no difficulty finding the rambling ranch house located on a small hill that Wade Smith had described. He got off the roan at the gate and led it in, going out to the rear where he could tie it up for his visit. He found a hitching post by the stable under a shady tree, then gave his attention to the rest of the grounds. Far to the right of the main house, there was a garden with fruit trees and waist-high hedges. There were two women strolling in it, and he was sure, even at a distance, that one of them was Virginia. He walked up the slight rise to the side entrance of the garden area and plainly recognized the brown-haired girl, who was in serious conversation with a tall, older woman dressed in black. When she saw him coming toward her, she smiled and ran to greet him.

'Sam!' she exclaimed with a smile. 'You have come after all. I was so worried that Father might have spoken to you and asked you not to.' She was dressed in something green and silken that set off her fresh young loveliness.

'I haven't talked to him since the funeral,' he said.

Now she studied his face with alarm. 'What's happened? You look as if you'd been badly beaten up!'

'That's exactly what happened,' he said. 'Last night.'

'You shouldn't have taken over as sheriff,' she worried. 'Not after what they did to Joel.'

'I've a lot to tell you,' he said. 'Is there some place we can talk?'

'There are benches down at the far end of the garden,' she said. 'You must say hello to my Aunt Cynthia first.'

She took him to the tall woman, her mother's sister. She was very charming, and there was a hint of Virginia's beauty in the older woman's face. Sam judged that it was from her mother that Virginia had inherited her looks and sweet nature. It was certainly not from the unprepossessing Charles Cameron! Aunt Cynthia welcomed him graciously, invited him to join them for the evening meal and stay overnight if he could. He thanked her, and then she discreetly excused herself and left them alone to find a bench at the other end of the garden.

Sam was pleased with the spot Virginia had suggested. It was isolated and pleasantly shaded by several tall apple trees. He sat with her and told her all that had happened since she had left Grant City.

She frowned when he mentioned Lean Jim Slade's murder. 'But what can this sudden rash of killings mean?' she asked.

He shrugged. 'Apparently they are tied in with the rustling that's been going on.'

She looked at him, her brown eyes showing distress. 'Father came out with some ridiculous statement that Joel was killed because he was helping the rustlers. I told him to his face that I didn't believe it.'

Sam's expression was solemn. 'He's spread the word all around Grant City. In fact, he's even tied me in with the outlaws. And Jim Halliday is helping him spread the lies.'

'But why?'

'Halliday is so mad about his herd being continually raided he's ready to believe any fool thing,' he told her. 'And your father seems to have deliberately set out to hurt Joel because he was against him marrying you.'

Virginia's pretty face grew somber, and she stared down at her wedding ring. 'Poor Joel!' she said softly.

He hesitated a moment before he plunged into what was bound to be the most difficult part of their talk. He said, 'Of course there could be another reason for him trying to throw suspicion on Joel.'

She glanced up at him in surprise. 'What?'

'He might be anxious to divert attention from himself.' His eyes met hers in a searching look. 'Have you ever wondered if your father might be mixed up in some crooked deal?'

'No, of course not!' she exclaimed. 'Why do you say that?'

'These things happen,' he pointed out quietly. 'He wouldn't be the first banker to finance and direct the operation of outlaws.'

'Dad wouldn't do a thing like that!'

'I hope not, for your sake,' he assured her soberly. 'But as sheriff, it is my job to look into every possibility.'

There was no mistaking the fear that shadowed her lovely face. 'You haven't found out anything to link him with the rustlers?' she asked in a low voice.

'Not yet,' he admitted. 'But there are some suspicious points I'll want to clear up before I can be sure he's innocent. I'd hoped you might be able to help me.'

'How?'

'Your father often has visitors to the house, people with whom he does business.'

She nodded. 'Of course.'

'Can you recall any dubious characters who may have come there after hours? Bull Bender, for instance? I assume you know him by sight.'

'Yes. But he has never been to our house. My father wouldn't have anything to do with a criminal like him.'

Sam listened patiently and made no comment. 'What about Slade?' he wanted to know. 'Did he ever visit your father?'

She looked guilty as she hesitated before replying. Then she admitted, 'Yes. He came to the house several times.'

'Did your father ever mention what his business with Slade was?'

'No,' she said. 'He never discusses business matters with me. But it could have had to do with the saloon. As you know, my father is executor of Bruce Thorpe's estate, and he has helped Laura manage the Grant City Saloon since his death.'

'You could be right,' Sam was willing to agree. 'I understand your father is already trying to purchase the Longhorn for Laura now that Slade is dead.'

'I'm sure whatever Jim Slade came to see Father about was a legal business matter,' she said.

'I want to think that as well,' Sam said with a sigh. 'I'm also determined to find out why Joel was murdered, and I'll continue to suspect everyone who could possibly have a motive until the mystery is solved.'

'I'd like to be able to help you,' she said unhappily. 'But I think you are making a mistake suspecting my father.'

He looked at her with sympathy. 'I can understand your feelings,' he said.

Virginia frowned. 'I know you don't like him,' she continued. 'And I can't blame you for that. There are times when I hate him myself, so I can't expect strangers to understand him. He's a mean man, even a cruel man. But I know he'd never involve himself in anything like murder.'

'Perhaps you're right,' he said gently, although he was still by no means convinced in his own mind. 'I wanted to make this visit, anyway.'

'And I have been longing for you to come.'

'When this is all behind us,' he said, 'the sadness and the violence, perhaps we can think of the future again.'

Virginia sighed and looked down at her wedding ring. 'I hope so,' she said in a whisper.

'Right now it's like a nightmare that has no ending,' he said. 'But if we can somehow survive it, I'll never make the mistake of leaving you again.'

She raised her eyes to meet his, and there were tears in them. But there was also a tremulous smile on her lips. 'It will be all right, Sam,' she whispered. 'It has to be!'

And then, because it seemed right, he took her in his arms for a brief kiss.

Later, they strolled back to the house hand

in hand and joined her Aunt Cynthia for dinner. Sam enjoyed the company of the two women and lingered for a while afterward. Then he excused himself, explaining that he had to return to Grant City before it got too late. Virginia was reluctant to see him go but understood his reasons. She went to the gate with him and stood watching until he rode out of sight.

The sun had gone down, and the unpleasant heat Sam had experienced on the ride over had given way to a cool evening. He made good time on the lonely road and for some time met no one.

It was when he came to a section of rolling hills with high boulders and clusters of thick bushes that he began to experience the strange feeling that he was being followed. He had not heard the sound of hoofbeats or seen a rider, but again that sixth sense of his came into play. He urged the roan on to a faster speed and at the same time gave furtive glances to his left and right.

There was a string of hills with giant boulders to his left, and he knew it would offer an ideal hiding place for anyone shadowing him. He gave this area his special attention as he drew his Colt from its holster and held it ready.

Then suddenly the head and shoulders of a rider showed above a tall boulder, and he saw a rifle fixed on him. A moment later a shot rang out, and then another in quick succession. The second one came whizzing close to him. At the same instant the roan stumbled, and Sam, caught unawares, pitched from the saddle onto the ground. He lay there stunned for a moment as the roan came to a halt and stood uneasily a short distance away from him. He knew his unknown assailant on the rocks above had a perfect target now, and he lay very still. It was just possible the man who'd fired at him would think he'd been hit. In fact, his best hope was to play dead and wait to see what would happen.

He had lost the Colt when he fell and now gradually reached out a hand to grasp it and draw it close to him. This done, he lay completely still and hoped his would-be killer would ride off. But it didn't work out that way. His nerves went taut as he heard the sound of a horse coming close, and he had to make a great effort to force himself to remain motionless. He opened his eyes just a slit to try to see what was happening.

The rider came to a halt nearby, and the dust raised by his horse drifted across to where Sam lay and almost made him sneeze. He knew he had to resist the impulse or he would be done for. Through slitted eyes he watched the rider dismount and come slowly toward him with his rifle still in hand. Then the killer was standing directly over him with a sneering smile on his face. And he saw that it was Bull Bender!

CHAPTER ELEVEN

The vicious, beetle-browed outlaw's rough-hewn features registered an expression of utter hatred as he stood over Sam's prostrate body. Then very slowly he raised the rifle and took aim to drill Sam at close range and make sure he was properly finished. Sam had been holding his breath, careful not to move a single muscle, but all his instincts warned him that this was the moment.

He sprang forward and grasped the outlaw around the knees, toppling him to the hard earth. Bender gave a grunt of surprise as he fell, and the rifle went off, its bullet spending itself harmlessly in the air. Before the fallen man could recover, Sam had wrested the weapon from his grip and thrown it aside.

Bull Bender's pockmarked face was a purple picture of rage as he clawed out at him. Sam had made the most of his advantage of surprise, and now it was going to be a more even battle. He was unable to prevent the outlaw from struggling to his feet again, but quickly hooked an arm around his neck, flipped an ankle behind him, and pounded the ugly face of the man who'd tried to kill him. He shoved Bender backwards and hooked his left elbow into his face.

Bender staggered, but came at him again at once, breathing heavily, his ugly face covered with perspiration, flailing away with his great fists. Sam took some punishment and then landed a right to the outlaw's jaw that sent Bull sprawling. The outlaw kicked at him viciously from the ground and almost caught him. Then Bender was on his feet again. He came at Sam with a renewed energy born of his fury. They exchanged brutal blows to face and body; then Bender took from Sam a heavy left jab that staggered him to his knees. He crouched there for a moment as Sam moved warily, ready for the next assault. This time it was Bull Bender who pulled the surprise. He leaped forward not at Sam but toward the Colt, which he swept up from the ground with a wild cry of triumph.

Sam knew this could be the end for him. He had no choice but to hurl himself on the outlaw. They both fell and rolled on the rocky ground as Sam vainly tried to wrest the weapon from Bender. It went off, and the noise of its explosion and the searing heat of its fire only heightened the mad life and death struggle between the two men. Then there was a second, rather muffled report, and in the same instant a surprised expression crossed Bull Bender's rough-hewn face and he suddenly went limp.

Rising slowly over his opponent's motionless body, Sam soon saw the reason. Bull's belly was a mess where the bullet from the Colt had ripped into him. With a grim expression on his thinly handsome face, Sam forced himself to take in the details of the wound; the oozing bloody gash left no doubt that all life had ebbed from the outlaw's body. The Colt had slipped from Bender's lifeless fingers, and Sam bent down and retrieved it.

Actually, he had not wanted to kill Bender. He would have much preferred to take him into Grant City, let him stand trial and answer for his crimes in the manner prescribed by law. In this way he would have been able to question the outlaw and perhaps have found out the whole story behind the rustling. If Bender had a superior who was directing the operation, he might have divulged his identity in a bid to win clemency for himself. Now there was no hope of that. Bender's lips were sealed for all time. If he possessed any secrets, they had died with him.

He led the outlaw's horse back to where Bender lay and lifted the dead weight of the outlaw's burly body across the saddle. When he had securely tied it in place and retrieved the rifle, he swung up on the roan and began the ride back to Grant City, leading the other horse with its gruesome burden.

It was dark when he reached the jail. Deputy Wade Smith came out in the doorway at the sound of his approach. The old man peered out at him with his failing eyes.

'You ran into some action!' he exclaimed.

Sam had dismounted and was about to untie Bender's body from the saddle. 'Plenty!' he said. 'You don't have to keep a lookout for Bull Bender any more. He's been taken care of.'

The veteran deputy came across the verandah and down the wooden steps to help him with the body. 'What do you know!' he said in an awed tone. 'How did you come to catch up with him?'

Sam told him briefly as they worked. Then they carried the body inside and put it on the cot. Sam made a quick examination of the contents of the dead man's pockets but came up with little that was unusual. However, there was one dirty scrap of paper which, unfolded, revealed a list of four names scrawled in a rough hand.

Sam frowned as he red the list: 'Simpson, Brown, Gale, Jeffries.' It meant nothing to him, but he stuffed it in his shirt pocket for further reference. Then he turned to Deputy Wade Smith. 'I reckon the next thing to do is notify the undertaker.'

It was nearing ten when Sam rode into town and stopped by the undertaker's place to notify the old man he had another customer. The undertaker could hardly believe his good fortune, it being his second unexpected windfall within twenty-four hours. His first, Lean Jim Slade, lay in cold silence in the front room of the establishment in one of the finest silver-handled caskets. He promised Sam he would go over to the jail with his wagon and pick up the body at once.

This being settled, Sam rode on to the mayor's office, knowing that Steve Randall often pored over his law books until midnight. But on this particular night the office was locked. The Longhorn was also in darkness, as the manager had decided it would be proper to shut it down until Slade was buried the following morning. As a result, Laura Thorpe's Grant City Saloon was especially crowded and busy.

Sam made his way through the noisy throng in search of Laura, but she didn't seem to be anywhere in the big room. The bar was crowded, so he decided to try her private office. He went down and knocked on the door, and at once her voice called from inside, inviting him to open it and come in.

He did as she told him and entered the pleasant little office to find Laura sitting at her desk with banker Charles Cameron seated across from her. Laura gave him a knowing smile. 'Well, I didn't think you'd return to Grant City tonight.'

Sam's eyebrows rose. 'Why do you say that?'

She shrugged. 'I expected the company in Arvilla would be too pleasant for you to think of leaving.'

'How did you know I was in Arvilla?' His tone was sharp.

Laura's pretty face wore a teasing smile. 'The stage driver told me he met you on the way there.'

So that was how Bender's employer had known! He was about to make a reply when Charles Cameron rose from his chair with a glowering expression on his puffy face. The banker pointed a pudgy forefinger at him. 'You went to see Virginia, of course! I thought I warned you to keep away from my daughter.'

'Virginia seemed glad enough to see me,' Sam said with a cold smile.

'Her judgment is nearly always bad in such matters!' Cameron snapped.

'We are old friends. I have a right to talk with her whenever she is willing to see me.'

The stout man was infuriated. 'We'll see about that,' he raged. 'I'll have a serious talk with that young lady!'

'Virginia is of age,' Sam reminded her father. 'And I think she is capable of knowing her own mind and choosing her friends.'

'I suppose you've been trying to turn her against me!' Charles Cameron said.

Sam shook his head. 'I'd say Virginia understands you perfectly,' he said. 'I don't know that there's anything I could add to her information.' He hesitated. 'I had other business in Arvilla, in any case.'

Laura Thorpe, looking very striking in a bright yellow gown, rose and came around the desk to him. 'You don't expect us to believe that!'

Sam's eyes met hers in a serious glance. 'Maybe you will when I tell you I brought Bull Bender back with me. His body, that is. He's dead.'

The lovely redhead showed surprise, but Charles Cameron looked even more startled when Sam turned to him. The stout man's puffy face went ashen-pale, and he seemed at a loss for words.

'You finally caught up with him,' he said at last.

'In a way, he was the one who caught up with me,' Sam said with irony. 'But I guess it amounts to the same thing. I settled with him.'

'What about Ramez and Samson?' Laura asked. 'From all accounts, they were the two with him when he shot down Joel.'

'He was on his own tonight,' Sam said. 'I still have to find them.'

'It might be more to your credit if you tried to locate them instead of wasting your time bothering my daughter,' Charles Cameron said, recovered somewhat from his surprise.

'I don't figure my time with Virginia was wasted,' Sam assured the banker in an easy drawl. 'And I aim to get those other two one of these days.'

Laura gave Charles Cameron a mocking smile. 'You'd better give up, Cameron,' she advised. 'I'd say Virginia and Sam are in love, and there's nothing you can do about it.'

The banker seemed ready to explode with rage, but before he could make any answer the door of the private office burst open and the hulking frame of Ben Halliday appeared in the doorway. As soon as the young bully saw Sam standing there, he showed consternation.

Laura Thorpe was the first to speak. In an annoyed voice she asked, 'Something I can do for you, Ben?'

He stared at her in a dazed manner. 'No,' he said finally. 'I just wanted to talk a mite. I'll come by later when you're not busy.' It was a lame speech and not like his usual arrogant approach.

Charles Cameron merely scowled at the intruder. But Sam had the feeling the banker might be secretly cursing the ranch owner's son for his stupidity in rushing in without first making sure who was in the office.

Laura smiled at the uneasy Ben. 'Come back in an hour or so,' she said.

Ben nodded. 'I'll do that,' he promised,

and left, closing the door after him.

'I expect he's missing the game at the Longhorn, which is closed tonight,' she told Sam. 'As a rule he spends some time at the table there every night.'

'Is it true he was deeply in debt to Slade?' Sam asked.

Laura shrugged her shapely shoulders. 'How would I know?'

Sam could have told her, but since she preferred to pretend to have no knowledge of the matter, he decided to let it go at that.

He gave Laura a thin smile. 'I reckon you two have some business to finish,' he said. 'I've got to be on my way.'

Laura's eyes held a taunting gleam. 'You're sure there is nothing else you want to tell me, Sheriff?'

'If there is, it can wait,' he assured her with a wise smile. And then, without even bothering to nod at Charles Cameron, he went out.

The crowd in the saloon was as large as before and just as noisy. Feeling thirsty, he made his way to the bar and elbowed himself a place. Within a few minutes the harried bartender managed to serve him a double whiskey.

After draining his drink, he made his way out of the saloon and back to the street. The first thing he noticed was there were lights in the mayor's office now. He decided to go over and talk with him.

After waiting for a wagon to pass, he crossed the street and walked up the board sidewalk as far as the mayor's office. He opened the street door and went inside, only to discover that the door leading to the inner office was closed. As he went toward it, he thought he heard a strange rustling sound and instinctively reached for his Colt and had it ready as he moved slowly to the private office.

He touched the knob and turned it, opening the door. But he was not prepared for the sight that met him. Mayor Steve Randall was tied and gagged in his chair. His eyes met Sam's in frantic appeal.

Sam gave a low whistle and crossed over to him. 'Looks like I'm a little late,' he said.

The mayor looked up at him with a strange expression as he struggled futilely to speak through the dirty rag stretched tightly across his mouth. Sam reached to remove it, and only then did it occur to him whoever had done this to the mayor might still be lurking there in the dimly lighted office. He was about to turn when something crashed down on the base of his skull and sent him falling into darkness . . .

When he came to, he was stretched out on the floor, and his head ached painfully. With a groan he raised himself a little and saw that the mayor was still a prisoner in the swivel chair behind his desk. He reached up to the desk for support and struggled to his feet. Glancing around, he saw that whoever had been lurking behind the office door had fled and that the room was deserted now. Strangely enough, his Colt was at his feet where he'd dropped it. Risking more pain from his head, he bent and picked it up.

'With you in a minute,' he murmured to the mayor as he moved toward the office door with a grim expression and the Colt ready.

He could have saved himself the time and trouble. The outer office was empty, as were each of several closets. He even checked a back room used for storage and found no one there. This done, he returned to the mayor and belatedly set about untying him.

'Should have taken a better look around when I first came in instead of rushing over to help you,' he said. 'I guess seeing you this way gave me such a start I didn't think of anything else.'

As he drew the filthy cloth from the mayor's mouth, Steve Randall said, 'I tried to warn you with my eyes. He was right behind you!'

'Who?' Sam asked as he went after the rope that was cutting into the mayor's wrists.

'Some Mexican,' Steve Randall said. 'There was another tough with him, but he left before you arrived.'

'What were they after?'

The mayor made a weak effort to stand and

tottered slightly as Sam cut free the last of the ropes binding him. 'I had the safe open. I don't know what they took.'

Sam noted that the contents of the ancient iron safe had been ransacked and that a lot of papers were scattered on the floor before its open door. 'They managed to make some mess of it,' he said.

The mayor left him and knelt down in front of the safe. After a moment he announced, 'My cash box is gone. You'd expect that! Luckily there wasn't too much in it. And the only other item that appears to be missing is a strongbox I received only today containing a collection of Jim Slade's personal papers. I hadn't even had time to examine them.' He sorted through the papers strewn on the floor as he spoke.

'It sounds as if that must have been the main thing they were after,' Sam suggested. 'Otherwise, why would they have taken only it and the cash?'

The mayor sighed as he rose, his hands filled with legal documents which he placed on his desk. He shook his head. 'It will take some time to clear up this damage,' he said. And then, as if he'd suddenly been able to focus his thoughts, he offered Sam a knowing glance. 'You're right, of course. It must have been Slade's papers they were after. Otherwise, why would the robbery have been timed so neatly for tonight? And what do you suppose is in that box?'

'Seems as if there may be some information in it somebody doesn't want you to discover,' Sam said.

'So they came for it before I could look over the material.' The mayor nodded. 'They probably planned to rob the place when I was gone. I came back because I had met the undertaker, and he told me about you drilling Bull Bender.'

'You weren't here when I came by the first time,' Sam said.

'I made a mistake in returning later.' He eyed the place with an air of weariness. 'I never expected anything like this to happen. They walked in on me with drawn guns.'

'You have no idea who they were?'

The mayor shook his head. 'No, except for the fact one of them was a Mexican.'

'Sounds as if it could be Carlos Ramez,' Sam said.

The mayor showed interest. 'Who is he?'

'One of the men with Bender when he shot my brother,' Sam said. 'Your other robber could be Samson, who was the third of the trio.'

'Well, at least we don't have to worry about Bender any more,' the mayor said. 'Did you manage to get him to talk before he died?'

'We were fighting when it happened. He went out fast. I hadn't time to put any questions to him.'

Mayor Randall sank into his chair with a sigh. 'Too bad,' he said. And with a shrewd look at Sam: 'Do you really think there is a higher up Bull Bender was answering to?'

Sam nodded. 'More than ever. Probably this robbery was carried out on his instructions.'

'Then unless we get to whoever it is, we're not much farther ahead,' the mayor suggested.

'We've gotten nowhere,' Sam admitted bitterly. 'They might stay quiet for a time just to put us off-guard, and then the whole thing will be organized again, and the rustling will go on the same as before.'

'A pretty hopeless picture, isn't it?'

'It's been that way ever since Joel was shot,' Sam said. 'But I figure if we can hold in long enough, whoever it is will be bound to overstep, and then we will be able to move in and really clean things up.'

'I'd like to believe you are right,' the mayor said.

'I'll hang on until you get the worst of this mess cleared up,' Sam said.

'No need,' the mayor assured him with a worn smile. 'Those people have gotten what they wanted. I won't be bothered again tonight.'

It turned out that the mayor was right. Things were quiet in Grant City for the rest of the night. The small elation Sam had felt over his bringing in Bull Bender was more than balanced by his chagrin at not having been able to question the outlaw and his failure to catch the robbers who had stolen the cash and Slade's strongbox from the mayor. He had walked into the trap they had set for him like an amateur and had let them get away.

He was still berating himself when he attended Lean Jim Slade's funeral the next morning. There was a good crowd there, but Sam kept aloof from everyone. His thoughts were concentrated on trying to remember some of the hints the dead gambler had given him, aside from the names of the outlaws who had killed his brother. Slade had definitely stated there was a higher-up in the rustling. And he had made it plain the higher-up could pay him well enough to make it worth his while to keep silent. He had also mentioned that he was cooperating with Sam because this could be profitable for him in the event a pay-off was refused.

The service ended, and Sam headed back to mount his roan. On the way he was intercepted by Jack O'Rorke, the farmers' representative. The small man smiled at him. 'I hear we're minus another of our less desirable citizens, Sheriff. You did good work in finishing off Bender.'

'I'd have been more satisfied if I could have gotten him to talk,' Sam said seriously.

The farmers' man eyed him curiously. 'You

don't think the rustling will stop now that Bender's gone?'

'I'm not sure that it will,' Sam admitted honestly.

O'Rorke looked gloomy. 'That's bad news, Sheriff. That gang has been getting bolder and greedier all the time.'

'They've hit some of you smaller fellows lately, I know,' Sam said.

The other man nodded. 'We were worried even when the Circle 3 was the only target, because we knew they'd get around to us sooner or later. Last time they cleaned up half the herds of two of our crowd.'

Sam nodded and sighed. He noted Charles Cameron driving off with Laura Thorpe in his carriage. Those two had been getting real friendly lately. He glanced around to see if there was any sign of Ben Halliday, but he wasn't among the group still standing near the grave. However, big Jim Halliday was there, talking earnestly to the mayor. Sam had an idea the big man might be discussing him, and if that was the case he knew the conversation couldn't be too pleasant.

'Keep me in touch, Sheriff,' Jack O'Rorke said, breaking into Sam's reverie.

'Depend on that,' he promised.

The little man nodded and walked on as Sam continued toward the post where his roan was hitched. Suddenly he remembered something and decided it might be worth mentioning to O'Rorke. He turned and hurried to catch up with the farmers' man.

O'Rorke was just about to step up onto his wagon when Sam called out his name. The farmers' man turned with a surprised expression and, seeing who it was, waited for him.

Sam came up to the wagon slightly out of breath. Reaching in his shirt pocket, he drew out the slip of paper he'd taken from Bull Bender. He said, 'I wanted you to take a look at this,' and handed it to him.

O'Rorke took the soiled square of paper and studied it. Then he gave Sam a curious glance. 'Where did this come from?'

'I took it from Bender's pocket after he died,' Sam said. 'Do those names mean anything to you?'

Jack O'Rorke nodded grimly. 'They sure do, Sheriff. Simpson and Brown were the two farmers who were raided last time. It looks like Gale and Jeffries might be next on the list.'

Sam whistled softly. 'It could be Bender has talked to us, whether he meant to or not!'

CHAPTER TWELVE

Jack O'Rorke handed the paper back to Sam. 'I know what you mean, Sheriff. The big problem is what to do about it. There may never be any more cattle raids now. Or if they do come, it may not be for a long time.'

Sam shook his head. 'I think different. It's my guess the big boss will hit again soon, thinking we'll be off-guard. I predict the next rustling will come within a few days.'

The farmers' man showed concern. 'You may be right, Sheriff. You make the theory sound convincing. I still say, what do we do?'

'A while back I asked you if you could provide me with a dozen good men on short notice,' he said. 'You told me you could. Does that offer still stand?'

'If it's to provide protection against the rustling, it does.'

Sam said, 'Here's what I want you to do. Round up the men and send half of them to stand special guard on the Gale herd and the other half to the Jeffries farm. Have a messenger ready at each spread to call on the other one for help in case one of them is struck. Do you think you can arrange that?'

'When do you want the men to stand guard?'

'By tonight, if possible,' he told O'Rorke. 'You'll keep in touch with what is happening and notify me in case of trouble. I'll be standing close by, in any event.'

'I think I can round up the boys for tonight,' the farmers' man said after giving it some thought. He glanced at Sam. 'There is one thing in our favor. Both the farms are fairly close to each other and not too far from town.'

'You can give me the exact layout later,' Sam said. 'And one other thing: I don't want this talked about. Bind all the men you enlist to secrecy. And see they keep undercover when they go to the farms.'

O'Rorke nodded. 'How long do you want them to stand guard?'

'Until the rustlers come,' Sam said. 'Not less than a week, anyway. By that time we can see what the situation looks like.'

Jack O'Rorke sighed. 'It's a big order, Sheriff. But I think they'll agree. I'll explain to them it's our only sure protection against the rustlers.'

'Do that,' Sam urged. 'And come by the jail this afternoon to let me know how you're making out.'

Sam rode into town, intending to see the mayor and tell him about the list. But then he changed his mind. With the theft of last night, the mayor already had enough to occupy him. There was nothing he could do to help the cause, and it might be in the best interests of secrecy to say nothing to him. That way there would be no temptation for the mayor to discuss their plan of action with big Jim Halliday or anyone else.

Instead, Sam went directly to the doctor's house. The doctor was out on a call but his wife allowed him to go in and visit a few minutes with Soak Dooley. Sam could see at a glance that the little man was in much better shape. Also, the doctor's wife had assured him that Soak's leg was on the mend.

The little man grinned. 'Guess I won't have to be a one-legged critter after all.'

'I'll have you back in the saddle again in no time,' Sam said. And he went on to tell Soak about his run-in with Bender and what had followed, being careful to omit any mention of the slip of paper with its list of names.

Soak leaned back against the pillows. 'Good riddance!' was his comment on Bull Bender. 'Looks like you've just about finished your job.'

'There are still the other two,' Sam reminded the little man. 'And I aim to put an end to the rustling as well before I turn in this star.'

'Bender was the main one,' Soak said. 'With him out of the way, you shouldn't have any more trouble.'

'I'd like to be that optimistic,' Sam said, 'but I can't be.'

The little deputy's purple face showed concern. 'You think there's still somebody heading up the rustling?'

'I'm certain of it.'

'One thing I've got to admit,' Soak said; 'your hunches generally turn out to be right.'

As the day wore on, Sam had reason to

wonder if Soak's words had any truth in them. He paced nervously up and down the jail office, while Deputy Wade Smith watched him with troubled eyes. The old deputy couldn't quite figure out what was in the air, and Sam wasn't about to tell him. By four o'clock, Jack O'Rorke hadn't come by with any report, and Sam began to think his whole scheme was doomed to failure. The farmers and ranchers were going to follow the line of thinking the rustlers wanted them to follow. They would assume that with Bender's death they were safe, and so leave themselves open to a surprise attack.

But a few minutes before five, O'Rorke rode up. When he came in, Sam saw that the dark suit of the farmers' representative was covered with dust. He must have been on the road most of the day.

O'Rorke collapsed in a chair and smiled up at him. 'It's all set, Sheriff,' he said. 'The men are rounded up and on duty right now.'

Sam studied the man's pleasant face with its lines of weariness and knew O'Rorke had gone out of his way to do his end of things well. 'Congratulations,' he said. 'I have an idea none of them is going to regret going to this extra effort. Or you, either, O'Rorke.'

The farmers' man sighed. 'All I hope is that, if they're coming they'll show up soon. The boys are bound to get tired of waiting around, and later on it may be hard to keep them in line if there's no action.'

'I'm counting on action,' Sam told him, 'plenty of it.'

But three days passed, and the rustlers didn't strike. Then it was the fourth day, and still there was no sign of them. On the fifth day, O'Rorke came to Sam and told him most of the men had voted to return to their own farms.

'If they do that, they're liable to wake up one morning and regret it,' Sam advised him.

O'Rorke looked unhappy. 'I've warned them,' he said, with a despairing gesture. 'But you know how impatient men can be. They think the danger is past and we're crying wolf for nothing.'

'Try and keep them on a few days longer,' Sam said, his handsome face showing the strain of waiting. 'Just a few more days.'

'I'll make them last the week as they promised,' O'Rorke said. 'But I'll be honest, Sheriff. If nothing happens by then, it's likely they'll just straggle back to their farms.'

The sixth day came, and still there was no strike by the rustlers. On the late evening of the seventh day, when Sam was seated at the table in the small kitchen off the jail office, having a snack with Deputy Wade Smith, a rider came pounding down the road at a wild rate. Sam heard the thundering hoofbeats, jumped up from the table and hurried out to the office to greet the rider.

The newcomer was wild with excitement. 'Come quick!' he cried. 'Hell has broke loose at the Jeffries' place!'

Sam reached for this gun belt and buckled it as he joined the other man in a race for the door. 'Did you get word to the men at the Gale place?' Sam asked.

'O'Rorke has gone after them,' he said. 'The rustlers had half the Jeffries herd rounded up before we knew it and opened fire. We have them bottled up in the valley now, and if we get help we'll be able to hold them.'

Sam made no reply, because by this time he was springing into the roan's saddle and heading for the Jeffries farm. It was one of the largest of the farmers' spreads, and the rustlers would enjoy a fine haul if they got away with their strike. The night air was cool, and Sam and the other rider maintained a fast pace along the narrow winding road. There was no moon, but there were some stars, and it couldn't be called a really black night.

As they drew close to the valley, the sound of gunfire being exchanged came clearly through the night air. Sam and the other man eased their horses to a slower pace as they made their way down a steep incline, thick with evergreens, to join the other members of the posse, who had taken a position there to keep the rustlers from making a break for the narrow passage that meant freedom.

There was the uneasy lowing and movement of the cattle caught between the lines of fire. The rustlers had taken positions to the rear and right of the herd, and Sam knew that their strategy would be to stampede the cattle at a certain point and let the frightened animals serve as a battering ram to get them out of this tight spot.

He could make out the figures of other members of the posse as he reined the roan under a tall evergreen and, in its protection, drew his Colt to join them in offering resistance to the outlaws. But he had a feeling this wouldn't be enough.

'You got here!' It was O'Rorke who came riding up beside him.

Sam said, 'Yes. We've got to do something fast, or those cattle are going to panic and make a break for the pass.'

'Maybe some of us could go up to the ridge and come down behind the rustlers,' O'Rorke suggested.

'That won't help the general situation except for picking off one or two of them from behind,' Sam said grimly. 'We've got to make sure the cattle don't do their work for them.'

'How?'

A sudden thought hit him. He leaned toward O'Rorke excitedly. 'Take three or four men and gather whatever brush you can. It doesn't have to be a lot; just enough to set a small blaze in the pass. Once the cattle smell the smoke and see the fire, nothing will make them go through there.'

The farmers' man nodded. 'It'll work all right, but there's just one danger. The fire could spread and turn the valley into an inferno. Then we'd lose the cattle for sure!'

'It's a balance we'll have to take,' Sam said grimly.

O'Rorke rode off to carry out his instructions. In the murky blueness of the night, the brisk exchange of gunfire continued. So far there had been only one casualty among the posse, and they couldn't tell what damage, if any, had been inflicted on the rustlers.

It seemed only a short time later that Sam smelled smoke and turned to see a good-sized blaze streaking up in the pass. The frightened lowing of the cattle grew in volume, and they began to make a wild retreat back into the valley. The tables had been turned on the frantic rustlers, who fired futile shots at the herd and into the air in an effort to stop the wild rampage. It did no good. They had lost control of the cattle and their own hopes of escape.

Now the posse circled around the ridge and came down behind the outlaws. Within a half-hour all of the rustlers had been picked off by bullets or taken prisoner. This part of the operation completed, O'Rorke saw that the fire was brought under control and then extinguished.

It was close to midnight, and they were rounding up their prisoners, when O'Rorke took Sam aside. 'I've got some news that you'll be interested in,' he told Sam. 'Carlos Ramez was shot and killed, and his pal, Burt Samson, is down here, badly smashed up. A bullet got him, and then he fell in a spot where some cattled trampled him. I don't think he'll live to get to town. I thought you would want to see him.'

'Yes,' Sam said. 'Take me to him.'

One of the posse was kneeling by Samson, with a lantern on the ground nearby. When Sam approached, the posse member raised his head and shook it in an indication that the outlaw stretched out before him was a goner.

Sam bent over the injured man and was not able to recognize his battered pulp of a face. Hoping Samson would hear him, he said, 'It's the Sheriff. We're going to try to get you to a doctor, Samson. It may help save your neck from a rope if you'll tell us who is behind this.'

There was a slight movement on the part of the desperately injured man, and then he gave a gasping rattle of a cough. He seemed to be trying to speak, but some injury was choking him and making it impossible. Sam bent near to catch even a whisper.

Then the words came, hoarse and

disjointed and with halting breaks between them. He whispered, 'Wales—cabin—beyond the mine—ask—Laura Thorpe!' Next a shudder went through the battered body, and Samson became as still as death. There would be no more information coming from him.

Sam rose slowly. This should be enough, he decided. From the beginning, he had known that a good deal of the rustling had centered on the mine and the valley behind it, where stolen cattle had been hidden and the brands on them changed. He had not made as complete an exploration of the territory as he'd hoped to do because Soak had been so badly injured. Now he must head back there on his own. But first he would check Laura Thorpe and find out from her what she knew about the cabin beyond the mine which the outlaw had mentioned. Perhaps it had belonged to her late husband at one time, since he'd owned property all over the area.

Sam turned to O'Rorke. 'You can look after things here,' he said. 'See that the prisoners get in to the jail and that the injured ones get medical care. I'm going to ride directly into town. I've got someone to see.'

'He told you something useful, then?' O'Rorke asked.

'He gave me a name to try for further information,' Sam said. 'And I don't want to waste any time.'

It was nearly one o'clock when he rode up

to the Grant City Saloon. It was about ready to close, and the place had only a thin sprinkling of customers. Sam looked around but saw no sign of Laura Thorpe. He worried that she might already have gone home to bed. He went across to one of the bartenders.

'Where is Laura?' he asked.

The man shrugged and consulted the barman next to him. The fellow came over to eye Sam warily. 'I reckon it's all right to pass on the information to you, Sheriff,' he said. 'She went out of town today to pay a visit.'

'Where?' Sam demanded, frustrated by the news.

'I ain't sure,' the barman said. 'Seems to me I heard her say something about going to Arvilla.'

It hit Sam hard. For no reason that he could properly understand, he was filled with a grave uneasiness. He was worried about what Laura might say to Virginia, whom she had undoubtedly gone to see; certain that she would do all she could to upset the grieving girl and turn her against him. He slowly made his way to the sidewalk and got into the saddle again.

Even though he was bone-tired and aching for sleep, he made up his mind he would move on to Arvilla at once. It would be almost dawn by the time he got there, but he would rather push himself and the roan beyond the point of endurance than merely sit around worrying and waiting for daylight. He wouldn't be able to settle down to a proper sleep, anyway, so he might as well spend the night in the saddle.

The first streaks of dawn were showing when he rode up to the ranch house owned by Virginia's aunt. It took some time to rouse a sleepy servant, and more time passed before Virginia's aunt came down to greet him in her dressing gown.

The older woman's eyes showed alarm. 'I hope there has been no trouble in Grant City, no more tragedy for Virginia to bear. Is her father all right?'

'As far as I know, ma'am,' Sam said politely. 'I apologize for waking you at this hour. But I need to speak with Virginia at once. I understand Laura Thorpe came to visit her yesterday.'

Virginia's aunt looked startled. 'No,' she said. 'Mrs. Thorpe did not come here. And Virginia isn't here, either.'

Again a stab of panic ran through Sam. 'Virginia's not here?' he echoed.

'No,' the older woman hurried on. 'She left last night with the blond man who came to tell her about her father's accident. That's why I asked you just now if he was all right.'

He was stunned. He looked at the worried woman with grim eyes. 'As far as I know, Virginia's father had no accident. This must have been some trick to get her away.'

'Oh, no!' The woman pressed a hand to her mouth and looked as if she might faint.

'Did you recognize the man?' he asked sharply. 'Did Virginia know him?'

'I don't think so.' Virginia's aunt seemed uncertain. 'She was so upset about her father she didn't really say much to me before she left.'

'Can you describe him?' Sam asked desperately.

The woman considered. 'He was blond, with funny bright eyes, and he had a gaunt, sick look about him.' She shook her head and seemed near tears. 'That's all I can tell you. I can't seem to think! Do you suppose Virginia is in some terrible trouble?'

'I hope not,' he said grimly, and started off. Then he turned to say, 'If Mrs. Thorpe does arrive, tell her what happened. She may be able to help.' And then he left.

He was soon on the trail again, heading for the hills beyond Grant City and Barney Wales' mine. He had watered the roan and given it a short rest while he'd worked out a plan in his mind. He had no idea who the blond man was, but he was certain he had not come as a messenger from Virginia's father. He was beginning to believe the man had been sent to pick her up by the rustlers. They planned to hold her as a hostage for some reason.

In all probability, the mysterious unknown

who was the organizer of the rustling operations was the one responsible for Virginia being kidnapped. And it was this conviction that spurred him on to revisit the mine. The dying rustler had clearly mentioned the mine, and so the headquarters of the outlaw operation must be located somewhere in its vicinity. He was betting that Virginia had been taken there by the blond man who had pretended to come from her father.

He regretted not having been able to speak to Laura Thorpe, since she would probably have been able to help him. Of course she must have gone somewhere else; the bartender had made a mistake about her visiting Arvilla on the wild goose chase, for otherwise he would have known what had happened.

It was mid-morning when Sam arrived at the clearing where Wales' cabin was located. The sun was beating down, and he was feeling all the accumulated weariness of the past twenty-four hours. He found the cabin as empty as before, and there was no sign that anyone had been there recently. He drank from the nearby spring and watered the roan again, then moved on in the direction of the mine.

Looking into the dark entrance, he experienced a feeling of eeriness as he remembered seeing Barney Wales alive for the last time in there. He recalled the maniacal behavior of the miner and how he had fallen or jumped to his death in the underground lake. A brief exploration of the mine's entrance indicated it was also deserted. He hadn't expected to find anyone there. He was certain there must be another retreat used by the rustlers; one located in or around the valley he'd visited when he'd been up there before. So he urged the roan up the narrow trail through the evergreens toward the ridge overlooking the valley.

This time he was careful not to ride in the open, but clung to the tall trees and underbrush for cover. There were no cattle in the valley. He did not expect to see any, after what had happened last night. And he wondered what the rustler leader's reaction would be when they did not arrive with the stolen herd.

He rode carefully, circling the valley, until directly ahead he saw a large cabin almost completely concealed by surrounding trees. It was located on a knoll with a good view of the valley and all the approaches to it. There was smoke coming from its chimney and horses tethered behind it—two horses that he could see and perhaps a third one. He brought the roan to a quick halt and, trembling with anticipation, stared at the cabin for a long moment.

Then he dismounted and, patting the silky

mane of the roan, tied it to a nearby pine. He drew his Colt and moved carefully through the underbrush, figuring that somewhere between here he was certain there would probably be a guard. A moment later he was proven right. The figure of a man carrying a rifle came slowly into view. Again Sam gave a gasp of disbelief!

The man with the rifle was Barney Wales!

But he had seen Barney Wales die in the mine! Or had he? Of course not! He had found the torch, and because he'd heard the scream and the splash of water, he'd assumed Wales had been killed. Instead, it had been merely one of a crafty series of tricks to throw intruders off the scent of the rustlers. So it was Barney Wales who was the rustlers' secret leader! This thought was followed at once by another one that argued he couldn't be. Wales was merely a henchman like the others. Sam was convinced that the leader was in that cabin and that he would find Virginia a prisoner there. But how could he get by Wales or bring him down without attracting the attention of whoever was in the cabin?

A bullet was out of the question. The shot would be heard. Sam watched as Wales came strolling in the open field only a short distance from him. He glanced down and saw that he was crouching on a bed of loose rock. Tentatively he lifted one of the stones. It was several inches in diameter, with cruel edges.

Would it serve as a weapon? He decided to take a desperate gamble and carefully drew back as he poised himself to hurl the rock with all the force at his command. He watched it fly through the air and saw it catch Wales directly on the cheekbone. His hands flew up protectively as the rifle was abandoned, and he fell forward silently onto the grass. Sam sprang forward and went over to him. He used the unconscious man's belt and neckerchief to secure his hands and feet, then gagged him with Sam's own neckerchief.

Not, he decided grimly, that Wales was likely to do any talking for a while. He was reasonably sure that, in addition to Wales' cheekbone being shattered, he also had a broken jaw. It would be some time before he could resume his role as a lunatic; not that there would be any point in the pretense now that the rustling was about to be ended.

Colt in hand, Sam dodged across the field, using boulders and brush for concealment as he went. At last he was at the cabin, and he slowly raised himself to a side window and stared into the big main room. The sight revealed to him was more unexpected and frightening than any he had encountered thus far.

Virginia was tied in a sitting position in a plain chair. She looked terrified. And across the fireplace from her stood Laura Thorpe!

Laura spoke, and he could hear her

through the partly opened window. The pretty widow was bitingly disdainful. 'You were a little fool to fall for that story about your father. Surely you should have guessed the truth before Barney got you here.'

Virginia was weakly defiant. 'You must be insane! Why have you done this?'

'Because you stand in my way. First you took Joel. Now you've won Sam from me. And I always have been in love with him. The boys will be here soon, and we'll start changing the brands on the cattle they bring with them.'

'You're the one behind the rustling?' Virginia sounded incredulous.

'That and a few other deals,' Laura said with a harsh laugh. 'I am not the weak feminine type, like you. I learned a long while ago that a woman can match a man when it comes to getting what she wants. I've been doing pretty well with this rustling. Sam finished Bender the other night, and I was glad to get him out of the way. The rustling will go on, with Ramez and Barney Wales as the leaders.'

Virginia stared at her. 'Then you ordered Joel killed?'

'On his wedding day, because he made a fool of me!' Laura mocked her. 'And when Lean Jim Slade found out he tried to blackmail me. So he had to go! Now it's your turn, and I have something special planned for you. I'm going to give you the Cactus 8 brand on each cheek, and then Barney will take you out somewhere and leave you for the vultures. Meanwhile I'll be sending the boys on to Abilene with the cattle, and I'll go back to Grant City and make my peace with Sam. He's bound to turn to me for consolation.' As Laura finished speaking, she went over to the fireplace and, taking a heavy cloth, used it as a wrapper to remove a glowing branding iron from the blazing logs. Holding it before her, she approached Virginia, saying, 'This won't improve your beauty, dear. But you'll not know. You'll be unconscious in a minute.' And very gradually, very deliberately, she closed in on the bound girl with the glowing iron.

Virginia uttered a scream of sheer horror and tried to free herself.

It was then that Sam broke the glass, and the startled Laura swung around to see who it was who had fired at her. He had meant only to hit her arm. It wasn't his fault that the lovely widow suddenly crouched and the bullet was embedded near her heart. Laura died in the same instant, although all that was decent in her must have perished long before that.

Sam was in the cabin in a matter of seconds. And only a few seconds more passed before he had Virginia freed and in his arms. He turned away from the body of the dead

Laura Thorpe, saying, 'Try to think of it as a nightmare. As time passes, that is what it will seem like to you. It's over now.' And he gently led her to the cabin door.

The sun was blazing, nature serene. Soon they would be in Grant City.

Photoset, printed and bound in Great Britain by
REDWOOD PRESS LIMITED, Melksham, Wiltshire